MY UNFAITHFUL

BABY DADDY

3

Rikenya Hunter

D1468374

Synopsis

After Zarela served Cinnamon a serious butt whipping, Cinnamon delivers a low blow to Zarela confessing that Cadel was secretly going for full custody of their son, Mayur. Will he follow through with his plan?

Cadel is known to flip-flop when it comes to his heart, will he have a change of heart and try to pursue Zarela one final time or will Cinnamon be the one woman for him? After suffering a pregnancy loss, can Ricardo and Zarela stay on track with their relationship? With Gabriela's mother Isadora sneaking back into Gabriela's life, can Zarela and Gabriela escape her wrath unharmed?

Take one final ride with Cadel and Zarela to find out on the finale of My Unfaithful Baby Daddy, a Baby Mama from Hell spin off!

~Acknowledgments~

First and foremost, I have to give praise to my almighty God! I'm truly blessed. God, I thank you!

To the love of my life, my fiancé Jeremy, I can't thank you enough for continuously believing in me. From high-school until now, you've been my rock and my backbone. Thank you for loving me. Thank you for listening to my crazy ideas and staying up late at night with me, keeping me company, when I'm on a writing challenge. When I mentioned wanting to write a book, you were right there supporting me, rereading my work and giving me ideas. Now, here we are on book number fourteen. Thank you for everything baby! I love you!

To my girls, Jayloni Queen, and Janai Princess, mommy loves you two very much! Always remember that you can do anything that you put your mind to, and I will ALWAYS support you two, no matter what!

Thank you, daddy, my sister Asia and my brother Desmond for always supporting me and loving me. I'm such a baby when it comes to writing these acknowledgments. I love y'all so much.

To my Auntietay, thank you for believing in me. I can't thank you enough for the continuous support. You've always been there for me and have never doubted me. You push me to become better at my craft each and every day. Words can't explain how grateful I am for you. I love you to pieces!

To my second mom, Linda, you're amazing, and you believe in me so much. You're always so excited when you see me writing or when a new book releases! You're a breath of fresh air and I adore you. You're the best, mom! I love you bunches!

To my readers and supporters, thank you for every comment, review, message and other types of feedback, I appreciate it! Major shout-out to Desiree Emory, Cara Waller, Sharon Thompson Lloyd, My God mother Latanya McCants and my sister in law, Tannisha Glaspie for the continuous support <3

To Niyah Moore: Even though our publishing relationship has ended, you're still very much a special person in my life. I thank you! <3

Please check out my other

titles:

My Unfaithful Baby Daddy

My Unfaithful Baby Daddy 2

Baby Mama from Hell

Baby Mama from Hell 2

Baby Mama from Hell 3

Patron On Ice (Anthology)

Outta My League

Unlucky In Love

Chapter 1

Zarela

"Are you surprised to see your mommy?" Isadora asked in her heavy Spanish accent.

Before we could react, Isadora and her sister forced themselves into Gaby's home as Isadora held a gun.

"Let's chat, shall we," Isadora asked, as she pointed the gun at us.

"How—how did you find me?" Gaby asked in a child-like voice.

It was as if Gaby turned into this scared little girl. I could see the fear and pain written over her face. I glanced at her mother and sister and knew that old bitch from the church was up to no good. I wanted to run up on these bitches but the cold hard steel Isadora was holding killed the idea.

I knew this wasn't going to turn out well. All I kept thinking was "Please let Paul hurry home!" I wanted to live to see my son tomorrow.

Isadora walked over towards the sofa as she continued to point the gun at Gaby and me. My heart was beating like an African drum. Isadora was a pretty woman but her ugly ways and cold heart made her unattractive. She and Gaby resembled each other, though. The only major difference was the few strands of gray hair poking around on Isadora's head.

"You know Gaby, sitting in that prison had me doing a lot of thinking. I know that I wasn't the best mother to you but I fuckin' did my best mi hija. I was a single mother trying to make ends me with four kids. I had no help from your sorry puta padre," she barked. She looked like a dog with Rabies with spit flying from her mouth and the evil, sick look that twinkled in her eyes. She continued talking when Gaby didn't respond. "Look at you, just staring at me like I'm crazy." Isadora chuckled as she stared back at Gaby.

"I'm looking at you crazy because you're holding a gun and pointing it at me and my best friend," Gaby said scared but sternly. Isadora scoffed and shook her head. She turned her attention to me as she just stared at me for a few seconds. No one said anything as she glanced from me to her daughter.

"So, who's your little friend? You didn't introduce me to her?" She stared at Gaby waiting for a response. When she noticed that Gabriela wasn't budging she continued talking.

"C'mon, Gabriela, introduce your mom to your little friend. I'm surprised that you finally got a new friend after all that bull shit you put Kimora through. Well, I'll introduce myself," she said slowly walking towards me.

"Hello. I'm Gaby's mother and you are?"She smiled at me wickedly and evilly. Seeing her smile instantly gave my body chills. I stared at her and debated if I should answer her crazy ass.

"I asked you a question!" Isadora shouted.

"I'm Zarela," I said bluntly, staring her down. I wanted to wipe the floor with this plantain eating bitch!

I was scared shitless on the inside with her holding this gun, though knowing she was crazy and loose of a few marbles but without that gun, I would for sure make her eat my hands. Everyone always had my hands fooled because I was skinny with a flat pancake ass, B cup breasts and had a proper voice but all that bull shit went out the window when I got pissed. I was like an African American Drita Davanzo when it came to my hands. Fuck with me and I would knock out your lights. I decided to keep my cool since this woman had bullets with her. My hands were fast but bullets were faster. I needed to play my role and play it smart.

"Zarela. That's a nice name," she said grinning. She glanced back at her daughter and instantly got pissed.

"Gaby if you don't stop staring at me like that, we're going to have a problem. You think you're so better than me because you have all of this? Newsflash, you're not better than me. You'll end up just like me."

"I won't end up like you. In case you hadn't noticed, I'm already doing better than you. I have a man that loves me and proposed to me. We're going to get married and raise our kids together," she said matter-of-factly.

"Oh really, where are my sons?" Isadora walked from the sofa and began walking through Gaby's house. Gaby and I stood in place since Isadora's sister kept an eye on us. After a minute of complete silence, Isadora returned into the living room.

"Nice place Gabriela," Isadora said sarcastically and rudely. She walked over to Gabriela's wine glass holder that sat on the kitchen counter. We eyed her from the living room since you could see inside the kitchen from where we stood. With the gun still pointing at us, she began to pick up wine glasses and toss them onto the ceramic tile floor. CLANK! WHAM! Pieces of shattered glass littered the floor as she continued to break each wine glass.

"STOP IT! Stop ruining my home. You're not welcomed here. Just leave!" Gaby shouted. I could tell she was growing angry and beginning to speak her mind. I just stood there, contemplating my next move. I kept my tongue in park because when I got mad my mouth could be lethal and I didn't know what type of tricks Isadora had in that bag because in that bag contained a gun.

"Oh, now this is the Gaby that I remember. Speak your mind my child." Isadora walked from out of the kitchen and back into the living room.

"I want you to leave. I want no parts of you in my life. You made me lose my daughter Mia. I could never forgive you for that," Gaby shouted with tears in her eyes. The tears slowly streamed down her face. I glanced at Isadora's sister and she just stood there, showing no emotion, just like her sister. These two old bitches were crazy.

"Cry me a river Gabriela," Isadora said in her thick Spanish accent. "I've come back for what's mine and that's my sons. If you wanna do suttin' about it, let's do it. You know I'll still pop off like fish batter." Isadora sat down on the sofa and kicked her feet up on her coffee table, kicking off coasters and remotes from the table. Once the coffee table was clear, she crossed her legs.

"I'm not going anywhere!" At that moment, we heard a key turning into the door. Isadora jumped up. Seconds later, Paul walked through the door.

"She's got a gun!" Gaby shouted.

I quickly ran towards Isadora, pulling her hair, since her back was turned to me. I grabbed her arm, as we wrestled for the gun. I felt a huge punch into the back of my head and realized that her old ass sister just sucker punched me.

"You bitch!" Gaby screamed as she charged at Isadora's sister. Gaby couldn't really fight for shit, so I'd hope she was getting the best of the old woman. Seconds later, Paul raced over and tried to pry the gun from Isadora's hand. She held a grip like a mother fucker.

POW! POW! POW! The gun went off three times before we were able to get it out of Isadora's hand. With the gun finally out of Isadora's hand, I hit her ass with a two piece that knocked her clean on her ass. I glanced over in shock to see a bullet hole through Isadora's sisters' head and next to her, Gaby laid with a bullet through her right shoulder. Blood was everywhere!

"AHHHHH," Gaby winced in pain. Slowly her wincing turned into screaming as she began to wail in pain and agony from the gunshot wound.

I ran to Gaby's aid as Paul at a fast pace called 911. Isadora was finally coming to her senses and realized that her sister had been killed. She tried to run to her sister's aid, but Paul quickly put her into a headlock with his free hand. She kicked, screaming and cursed him out in Spanish as she stopped fighting when tears fell from her eyes.

"Lo siento mucho…Lo siento mucho…Lo siento mucho," Isadora repeatedly cried out.

"Gaby, you're going to be okay. Paul is calling 911. You're going be fine," I kept reiterating as Gaby's eyes fluttered. There was so much blood that I couldn't tell how bad the wound actually was. I ran to the kitchen, ripping open drawer after drawer, trying to find a dish towel. In the background, I could hear Paul rattling off his address to the 911 operator as Isadora wept in the distance. *Serves that bitch right!*

I finally find a dish towel, snatch it in my grasp and run back to Gabriela. I stumble but quickly regain my composure. I kneel down and began applying pressure with the dish towel onto Gaby's wound. She was still in and out of consciousness.

"Gaby, baby girl, stay with me! Stay with me! You hear me. Stay with me Gabriela," I frantically shout. I quickly look over at Paul who's shouting to keep applying pressure as he hangs up the phone with the 911 operator. He continues to keep an eye on Isadora who's in shock and in tears at the death of her sister.

"You evil bitch! You killed my sister," Isadora hollers as she tries to charge at me, but to no use since Paul still had one arm wrapped around her neck.

"Oh please, I've been called worse by better. You're a sorry excuse for a mother," I yelled back with tears in my eyes.

"I should've given her up just like I did her sister Patricia. Her daddy told me that he wanted to raise her and become a family but he changed his mind, cheated and left me pregnant, just like all the others. I couldn't take the pain of looking at her without thinking of her father, so I put her up for adoption at birth. I should've just aborted Gabriela's ass and raised my sons because she's caused me nothing but pain and turmoil in my life," she screamed at Gabriela not knowing that Gaby was in and out of consciousness from the loss of blood and couldn't hear anything that she was saying.

"Shut the fuck up!" Paul yelled as he gripped her slightly tighter around her neck, causing her to shut the hell up. The sound of the sirens in the distance began to calm me down because I knew that help was on the way.

"Walk! Walk your ass out my motherfuckin' house bitch! They're gonna take your ass right back to prison and for life! How dare you bring your ass through my shit." Paul walked out of the condominium with Isadora still in his grasp. Within seconds, paramedics rushed inside and began tending to Gaby. Tears slowly rolled down my cheeks as I thought about my friend lying on the floor, dying. I wiped a tear from my eye as I walked outside. I couldn't stay inside any longer watching my best friend suffer.

Once outside, the air from the wind blowing instantly made me cold from all of the sweat stuck to my body. Chills ran over my body from the top of my head to the bottom of my feet. I stood on the top of the stairs and watched as police took Isadora into custody. She was kicking, screaming and crying as if she was the victim. I shook my head. That woman was unbelievable. My heart went out even more to Gaby having to grow up with her.

"I just wanted my sons! She has my boys! I just wanted my sons," Isadora whined as the back door to the police car closed in her face. I could still see her mouth moving as she sat in the back seat, crying and going off. That woman had some serious issues.

Paul raced to the top of the stairs, brushed past me and went inside his place to check on Gabriela. I stood in place and silently prayed that my best friend made it out alive and I even thanked God for keeping me safe and unharmed in this mess.

Chapter 2

Cadel

"See what the fuck you started! You always gotta run ya mouth Cinnamon. Sometimes you just need to let shit be man." I was furious as I drove down the street. Just thinking about the fight back at the gas station had me heated. I glanced from Cinnamon to the road and shook my head.

"Stop yelling at me! I was trying to defend you," Cinnamon shot back. She pulled down the sun visor and dabbed her nose with a tissue as she surveyed her injuries. Besides a few scratches, she looked okay. Her nose had stopped bleeding and she began to apply makeup to hide and conceal the scratch marks.

"I'm sorry baby. I didn't mean to yell at you but you have to realize that Zarela and I have a child together, so let our business be our business. You telling her about

my plans to take her to court were unnecessary C, for real."
I grabbed a rubber band and tied my dreads back as we sat
at a red light.

"Well, I'm sorry. Maybe I should've just let her get
in your face and beat your ass."

"Like she did you," I said, immediately regretting it.
Her neck swiveled around as she stared at me in disbelief.

"Really Cadel? You have to be kidding me. Why
are you faulting me for sticking up for you?" Cinnamon
asked. I ignored her and continued focusing on the road.
Cinnamon then applied two layers of clear lip gloss to her
succulent lips and pursed them together once she was
satisfied with the outcome.

"That bitch is gonna have to come harder than that
if she thinks that she was gonna fuck up my face,"
Cinnamon sucked her teeth and slammed the sun visor shut.

"Ay yo, watch how you treat my shit, Cinnamon. I don't play about my ride. I know you mad and all but you gonna have to chill baby. That shit that happened was crazy but it's over with. This is why we needed this vacation."

"Yeah, I suppose," Cinnamon added as she stared out of the window. She was mad, but she would get over it. I glanced down at my phone and noticed that the Department of Children and Families were calling again. I shook my head and hit ignored, letting the voicemail pick up the call.

"Who was that?" Cinnamon asked, being nosey.

"Nobody," I answered. I didn't deal with people questioning me and all in my business.

"Yeah, right, okay then," she responded, crossing her arms across her chest.

I ignored her as we eased onto I-95. I turned on the radio because after the fight and dealing with her attitude, she was killing my vibe. The sound of The Weeknd singing "Acquainted" filled the truck. It must've been Cinnamon's song because she turned up the volume knob and began singing along. All I could think about was her on stage, shaking her ass to this song. I chuckled at my thought.

"What's so funny?" She asked.

"Nothing, sing your song woman! Stop worrying about me," I joked. "Just relax because we're on our way to Miami!"

~

We arrived at Miami South Beach and it was our first time experiencing the city. I was lucky enough to score a hotel room on the beach. The sun was shining as people were walking around in bathing suits, two pieces and the most revealing outfits. I could smell the salt from the beach water through the car AC vents.

Even though we lived in Jacksonville, we'd never visited Miami. Just being in Miami for these few minutes you could already see the difference between the two cities. You could see why Miami was a vacation spot attraction. Miami Beach was quickly proving to already be a fantastic and eye-appealing and awe-inspiring place. With the Intracoastal Waterways, Biscayne Bay, Canals everywhere and the magnificent Atlantic Ocean of the East, Miami Beach was truly looking like paradise. I couldn't wait to see what all Miami had to offer.

I had booked us reservations at The Hotel of South Beach. I was low key excited. Cinnamon peered out the window like a little girl. I could see the twinkle of excitement in her eyes. We pulled up to the amazing hotel and Cinnamon almost broke her damn neck trying to get out of the car because she was so excited.

"Girl, slow down," I joked while laughing.

"No, speed up, old man! I'm ready to see what the city is offering."

Concierge approached us and helped us with our bags as we walked into the lobby of the hotel. The place was beautiful and for three hundred and ninety-nine dollars per night, it better be.

"Good evening, checking in?" The young female at the front desk asked. She looked like she was star struck as she stared at me with googly eyes. She tossed her curly black tresses behind her shoulder and smiled. In the corner of my right eye, I could see Cinnamon burning a hole into the young receptionist face. She didn't care though because she continued to smile at me, showing off her pearly white teeth.

"Yeah, checking in," I responded, licking my lips.

"Name please, sir," she asked sexily.

"Cadel Wright," Cinnamon interrupted rudely, answering for me. She shot me and the front desk clerk a look. I laughed on the inside because she was so damn jealous yet she stripped twenty-four seven in front of random dudes. Shit, I should be the jealous one.

"Okay, I see you right here, Mr. Wright," the bubbly receptionist said, only staring at me and ignoring Cinnamon as if she didn't just say my name for me.

"You have the "Summer in Love" package. As you know couples can enjoy South Beach's oceanfront breezes and star-studded evenings featuring chocolate covered strawberries, couples massages and much more."

"Wow, you went all out huh babe?" Cinnamon asked eagerly as she grabbed my arm, probably trying to make the receptionist jealous. Women were so crazy!

"In your room is complimentary welcome cocktail's. A bottle of red wine will be in your room upon arrival also. On your second night, chocolate covered strawberries will be delivered along with red rose petals. Your couples massage is an hour long. You two have two complimentary reserved beachside chaise lounges daily. Amenities include a rooftop pool and a vibrant bar and lounge with skyline views. There's also a casual cafe and an exercise room, plus reserved chaise lounges on the beach. Last but not least, you have complimentary Saturday morning Yoga."

"I'on know bout that yoga shit but a'ight shorty. Can we get the keys?" I felt like ole girl was talking too much to just try and keep me standing in front of her longer.

"Babe, just try the Yoga please, I'm sure you'll love it," Cinnamon laughed as she wrapped her arm around mine.

"Shittttt, like I said I'on know Cin," I said chuckling. Cinnamon began fake pouting as she poked her lips out. I ignored her and turned my attention to the front desk clerk.

"Well thank you, Jasmine," I said to the receptionist once she handed me our room keys. She smiled and wished us a great stay. Neither one of us replied and just walked off. She was thirsty as fuck.

We eased into the elevator and pressed our floor level. We were the only ones on the elevator and Cinnamon began to tug on my shirt, pulling me into her. I inhaled her fruity scent that bounced off her body and into my nose.

"Thank you, baby, for this getaway, you're the absolute best."

She pulled my head into her space and kissed me, slipping her tongue into my mouth. Her tongue felt like a cloud with how soft it twirled inside of my mouth. I grabbed her ass with my right hand and squeezed it tightly. The elevator door dinged and an old elderly couple walked inside. We broke our make out session and Cinnamon giggled. The elderly couple glanced in our direction but remained to mind their business. Once we arrived on our floor, I let Cinnamon walk in front of me and I slapped the shit out of her fat ass, causing it to jiggle.

We walked down the clean hallway and arrived at our hotel room door. I inserted the room key and held open the door for Cinnamon. She was in awe and I had to agree that the room was everything. The bright, Todd Oldman-designed suite featured a 39 inch flat-screen TV, mini-bar, Keurig coffeemaker and rainfall showerhead. The WiFi was free. We had an amazing balcony with an ocean view. We even had a living room.

"Wow babe! This is everything! There's a Jacuzzis in the bathroom!" I heard Cinnamon shout. She was running around the suite like a kid in a candy store. I was happy to see her happy.

I walked over to our complimentary cocktails and red wine. I quickly downed my girly ass cocktail and popped the bottle of red wine. I need something stronger than this little wimpy ass cocktail and fancy bottle of wine but this would do for now. I grabbed the corkscrew and popped open the bottle of wine. POP!!

I looked up and noticed Cinnamon sashaying out of the bathroom, butt naked. I had to do a double-take because she caught me off guard. Her big cantaloupe breasts bounced up and down as she strutted over towards my direction. I loved what I was seeing as I eyed her voluptuous and curvy body. All I saw was light skin and tattoos that decorated her body. I licked my lips and took the entire bottle of wine up to my lips and chugged some of the contents.

"Baby, you know that you like what you see," Cinnamon teased. She grabbed the bottle of wine from out of my hand and drunk from it, eyeing me the entire time.

"Damn right I do girl. Bring that ass here," I said taking the bottle out of her hand and sitting it back down.

I grabbed her around the waist and began sucking on her neck. Cinnamon untied my dreads letting them fall. She loved grabbing on my shit. I smacked her ass and began taking each peanut butter cookie nipple into my mouth. "Ahhh baby, you know that's my spot," she moaned.

I slid my hand down into her special spot and felt her stickiness sticking to my hand. I had her hot and wet. Cinnamon slowly backed away and walked over to the fluffy king sized bed. I eyed her as she lay back on the bed and began playing with herself. I licked my lips as I began undressing.

Within seconds, I stood in front of her in my boxers, gold chain and white socks. I walk over to the bed as Cinnamon grabbed me by the waist and yanked down my boxers. She immediately takes my thick erect dick into her warm mouth. I couldn't stop myself from moaning as I grabbed a fist full of her tracks that were sewed in. She forced every inch of me into her mouth.

I felt the tip of my dick hitting her tonsils. Cinnamon was slobbering and moaning as she continued to give me dome. I pulled my dick out of her mouth because I was about to cum fast like 911 in a white neighborhood. Cinnamon smiled devilishly as she licked her lips and began massaging my balls. She started jacking me off again then stopped as she began rubbing away the pre-cum with her thumb. I tugged on her weave as she mashed my hand away.

"Don't touch my weave daddy," she said, spitting on my third leg for more lubrication. She put her hand at the base of my dick and began to jack me off. I closed my eyes and just enjoyed the sensation of her jacking me off.

"Damn girl, stop," I uttered.

I push Cinnamon back onto the bed and spread her legs open. Cinnamon must of thought that I was about to put my lips on her second set of lips because she tried to push my head further down towards her pussy. She had another thing coming if she thought I was about to do that shit. Instead, I gently slid two of my fingers inside her warm cave.

"Oooh Cadel baby, yessss," Cinnamon moaned as I stroked her from the inside with my fingers in a come-hither motion. I felt her body trembling all over.

I got up from off the bed and went into my wallet and pulled out a golden ticket. She had another thing coming if she thought she was going to get dicked down raw. I glided on the condom and walked back over to her. I hovered over her body and slid inside of her.

"Ahhh," Cinnamon gasped. She wrapped her legs around my waist, securing me in between her thighs. She began nibbling on my ear and then hungrily sucked on my neck, leaving a hickey.

I started stroking her long, deep and on point as I hit every inch inside of her. Cinnamon kept her eyes on me the entire time, making direct eye contact with me. I watched as she bit down on her bottom lip because I was giving it to her so good. She began to match my thrusts and wrapped her legs tighter around my waist.

"Go deeper baby. I love it!" She screamed with bliss.

"See, I was trying not to hurt you," I teased.

I complied with her wishes and began to show her no mercy as my thrusts became deeper and harder. I watched her make the sexiest love faces I had ever seen. She began digging her nails into my back like a caged animal. "Damn girl," I muttered.

"Turn over!"

Cinnamon exhaled, out of breath and turned around. She tooted her cute ass up in the air. I slide into her center. Her pussy was farting and gripping me so tight. She felt like heaven. I could imagine how she felt with the condom off but I wasn't about to take that risk. I slapped her ass and kept one hand on the back of her neck while my other hand was gripping her waist. She tightened her pelvic muscles as I pounded in and out of her. She felt so good.

"Damn baby, beat this pussy up," Cinnamon moaned with her eyes shut.

The sound of the headboard banging into the wall and our skin slapping against each other was creating a rhythm that only could be heard along with our labored breathing. I for sure thought somebody would call the front desk and report the noise disturbance because we were in almost a four hundred dollars per night hotel room but at this moment, I didn't give a fuck.

"Damn girl, this mine? Does this shit---does this shit belong to me?" I groaned, pulling my lips together after my question.

It wasn't long before Cinnamon squirted all over the condom. That shit turned me on even more and I grabbed ahold of one of her breasts and massaged it. I felt myself tensing up because she reached underneath me and began massaging my balls.

"Ahhhh," I groaned as I released my babies into the latex. I pulled out of Cinnamon and collapsed onto the bed.

We were covered in sweat and the sheets were wet, covered in bodily fluids.

"Damn yo, that shit was bomb baby girl," I said out of breath.

I slowly got up from the bed and walked towards the bathroom. Inside the bathroom, I took off the condom and flushed it down the toilet. I began wiping off my shaft with a hot wash cloth. I wet another wash cloth and walked back towards the bed and tossed it to Cinnamon.

"Thank you," she said, doing a quick wipe down in the bed, before tossing the rag onto the floor. I eased back into bed with Cinnamon.

"That was so damn good Cadel," Cinnamon said, curling up next to me, laying her head on my chest. I nodded my head, too exhausted to speak.

We drifted off to sleep for a quick minute until Cinnamon's phone rang. I softly nudged her to let her know but she was in a deep slumber. I put her ass out like Nyquil. The ringing of her cell phone stopped so I closed my eyes and began falling back asleep myself. A few minutes later her cell phone began ringing again. I eased her off of my chest, careful not to wake her.

I walked over to her purse, dick swinging like Tarzan as I approached her purse and pulled out her cell phone, I glanced at the caller ID and saw the name Deon flashing on her screen. I instantly got pissed.

"Yo, Cinnamon, wake your ass up!" I barked, marching over towards her. Cinnamon stirred in her sleep and fluttered her eyes.

"Mane, get your ass up Cin," I yelled out as she slowly sat up, looking confused.

"Your phone was ringing."

"I know that you didn't just wake me up for my phone ringing, let the voicemail pick it up," Cinnamon whined as she lied back down and flung the covers over her head.

"Nah, get your ass up and look at who called," I shouted, veins popping out on the side of my neck as I flung the covers off of her body and onto the floor. Cinnamons eyebrows lowered and her mouth twisted up as she sat back up.

"Nigga what is wrong with you? Gimmie my phone," she said reaching for her cell phone. I gladly handed it to her. She glanced at her cell phone and sucked her teeth.

"Baby, I haven't talked to Deon in forever. You gotta trust me," she pleaded.

"Oh really, well let me see your call log then. Prove it!"

"I'm not playing this game with you," Cinnamon said as she swung her feet over the bed and stood up. I grabbed my boxers and quickly put them on.

"Yeah because your foul ass knows that you be creeping with other niggas man. I did all this shit for you and you still talking to niggas behind my back?" I followed behind her as she began putting on a blue and green Maxi dress.

"Cadel, I'm not creeping or cheating on you and you should know that. What you want me to do?" Cinnamon asked with pleading eyes.

"Quit the strip and go legit," I answered quickly.

"I can't do that. You know that I can't. I have to hustle. All I know is get money and money at the strip club is easy money baby. You gotta trust me." Cinnamon walked into the bathroom and began freshening up. I followed.

"I can't stop people from calling me who I once dealt with. I've had the same phone number for over five years."

"Well block his number then," I countered.

"Fine," she said rolling her eyes.

I stood there watching her admire herself in the large mirror that hung on the bathroom wall. "Just call me ranch because I am dressing," she joked as she began to touch up her hair.

"You think everything is a game with your corny ass," I chuckled.

Cinnamon joined in on the laughter and turned around, looking at me.

"We got something good daddy. I promise you I'm not trying to fuck it up. So, what are we about to eat?" She asked walking over towards me and wrapping her arms around my neck.

"I was thinking some Applebee's," I joked, knowing she hates Applebee's.

"Applebee's!" Cinnamon shrieked, dropping her arms from around my neck and staring at me.

"What? You too good for that Applebee's two for twenty menus but you know that your ass was raised on free lunch," I joked. Cinnamon cackled loudly. She was hardly able to catch her breath, from laughing so hard at my joke.

"Boy, you're crazy. After I finish, I'mma need you to go and get dressed so that we can go eat," she teased as she dropped to her knees and proceeded to show me what her mouth do with her freaky ass.

Chapter 3

Zarela

My heart was beating a mile a minute as I watched the paramedics hastily load an unconscious Gabriela into the back of the Ambulance. I glanced a few feet away and noticed them loading Isadora's sister's lifeless body into a body bag. Tiny raindrops started to fall onto my face as dark clouds rolled in. The sound of thunder roaring caused me to jump. Paul and I stood in the back of the ambulance as we watched them prep her for the ride to the hospital. Tears started to fall from my eyes as my tears began to mix with the rain drops.

"We can only take one person, so quickly whose riding?" The paramedic asked.

"He is."

"I am," Paul and I answered at the same time.

Paul jumped into the back of the ambulance as they started to sound off the sirens. I immediately ran to my car, jumped inside and proceeded to follow behind the ambulance who was dipping through traffic and running lights. I put on my flashers and prayed that I made it safely to the hospital since I was high-tailing it behind them.

After traveling a few blocks, we finally made it safely to the hospital. By now the rain was pouring down. I cut off the engine and jumped out of my car. Rain poured down on me as I ran inside the hospital emergency room and met up with Paul.

"What are they saying?" I asked nervously.

"We wait. They just took her back. Damn yo, this shit is crazy. What in the fuck happened?" I took a deep breath and I ran everything back, detail by detail to Paul. By the time I finished he was speechless.

"Yo, she was crazy as fuck. Gaby told me about her ass when we first got together. I bet her ass ain't getting out no time soon now. She's crazy as hell if she thought popping up with a gun and shit would get her the answers she wanted and seeing the boys." Paul shook his head and looked down at the floor. I noticed a single tear slip from his eye and land on his shirt. He swiftly wiped it away, hoping I wouldn't notice but I did.

"She's going to be okay Paul. Just stay positive," I whispered as I placed my hand on his shoulder. He promptly wiped his face again and looked at me.

"Thanks ma. I'mma go take a walk or something. I can't stand here like this," Paul said pacing.

"Okay, I'll be right here," I said with weary in my eyes. I yawned. I was exhausted but on pins and needles from everything that had happened.

"Yo," he said walking off with his head down. I know it was killing him that we didn't have any answers on Gabriela's condition but I needed to be strong for the both of us. I couldn't fall apart.

I glanced down at my phone when I heard it ringing. It was my baby Ricardo calling. With everything going on, he had no idea on what I had just gone through. I hurriedly answered his call and sat down in a chair. I was freezing cold with being drenched in the rain and then walking inside a cold air conditioned building. I shivered as I said hello into the receiver.

"Hey baby girl, I've been calling you. How are you?" Just from hearing the sound of his voice comforted me but also made me break down. All that "trying to be strong for Paul and I" went right out the window.

"Baby," I answered, voice cracking.

"What's wrong?" Ricardo asked concerned.

"Everything! I got into a fight with Cinnamon at the gas station. She ran off at the mouth that Cadel was trying to go for sole custody of Mayur. Can you believe that?"

"What? Are you kidding me? Sole custody for what?"

"Hell if I know! I whooped the shit outta her ass especially when I looked into the backseat of Cadel's truck and my son wasn't back there!" I yelled. I looked around, thankful that it wasn't too many people waiting inside the waiting room with me because I was loud.

"Where was he?" Ricardo asked eagerly.

"He's at his cousin Tawny's house. I located her and she wanted him to stay for a sleep over and would bring him home. So, fast forward a few hours later, Gabriela and I are taking shots of Patron and Gaby checks her mail and it's a suspicious letter from her mother saying that Gabriela and Pumpkin were sisters!"

"Sisters! Word? Man this is crazy Zarela. Is Gabriela okay?"

"That's the issue. Somehow her mother and crazy sister show up to the house, force themselves in with her mother holding a gun. Long story short, Paul arrives, Gaby gets shot in the shoulder and Gabriela's sister gets killed. Her mother was arrested on the spot. I'm at the hospital now with Paul. We don't know if Gabriela is going to be okay. Shit is so fucked up right now," I cried, not caring about who saw me.

"What hospital are you guys at? I'm flying out of the building now and I'm on my way." I rattled off the hospital we were at.

"Stop crying baby. Everything will be okay. Hold tight because I'm rolling to you now. I'll be there soon. I love you!"

"Okay," I mumbled as we hung up the phone. I stood up when I noticed Paul walking back in my direction. He handed me a can of Sprite.

"I thought you might be thirsty. Are you alright? Has the doctor came out and said anything?"

"Thank you," I said taking the can of Sprite from out of his hand.

"There haven't been any updates on Gaby. I wonder what's taking so long? I spoke to Ricardo and he's on his way out here."

"I don't know but they need to hurry up and tell us something before I go crazy," said Paul.

I nodded my head and popped the top on my can of Sprite. I chugged a big gulp of the soda and looked up when I saw a doctor approaching.

"Family for Gabriela Hernandez?" The doctor asked as he stood in the front of the room. He looked like he was stressed out. I tried to study his demeanor to see if I could read his body language on what he was about to inform us. His salt and pepper hair stood up on his head. He had stubble on his face which appeared that he needed a shave really soon. He appeared as if he hadn't slept in days. Paul and I stood up and walked over towards the doctor. I felt like I was walking on air and it felt like I was going to pass out as I braced myself for what the doctor was going to tell us.

"Hi, I'm Dr. Goldman," he said, firmly shaking our hands. "Gabriela is going to be fine. She's stable. We've removed the bullet and she's doing well in recovery. I do have to tell you that um…Gabriela is three months pregnant." Paul and I were stunned and stood before the doctor flabbergasted.

"Pregnant?" Paul mumbled.

"Yes, three months. So, congratulations! The baby is fine. Gabriela is sedated with pain medications that are safe for her and the baby. She's in recovery and you can go back and see her."

"But—wait, how this is even possible. We had no idea that she was pregnant. How could she not know?" Paul inquired.

"Well, every pregnancy is different. Sometimes you might not exhibit symptoms. It happens. Just be grateful that she and the baby are doing well. In a few more weeks, you'll be able to find out the gender. Now if you'll excuse me," he said shaking our hands and walking away.

I was so elated that my best friend was going to be okay and that she was recovering well. I was shocked that she was pregnant. Paul and I walked side by side as we made our way to Gabriela's hospital room. We knocked on the door and Paul slowly eased it open, letting me walk inside first. I took a deep breath as I cautiously approached Gabriela's bed.

"Gaby," I softly whispered into her ear. She stirred around and opened her eyes. The corners of her mouth slowly curled into a smile.

"I'm so glad that you're okay Gabriela. I was so nervous," I said, bending down and lightly hugging her. Silent tears slipped from my eyes as I just held my friend and thanked God that she was okay.

"Paul's here too," I interjected as I stepped back and turned around to see Paul walking towards Gabriela.

Gabriela immediately broke down into tears as Paul embraced and kissed her. Seeing them two together melted my heart. My best friend had a good man, was pregnant and was about to get married.

"Baby you know we're having a baby right?" Paul beamed. His face lit up as he placed his hands on his belly. Instantly, seeing how happy he was reminded me of the lost that I just had with Ricardo's baby.

"I still can't believe it! Are you excited?" Gaby asked whipping away her tears.

"Of course, I'm happy but you know we're going to need a bigger place with all these kids running around," Paul joked as he carefully sat down on the hospital bed with Gabriela.

"I know! Maybe after the wedding we could start looking for houses," Gabriela said eagerly.

"I like that a lot. I think that would be a good idea. For now, let's focus on making you Mrs. Gabriela Delgado." Gabriela grinned with so much excitement.

"I'm going to be an auntie," I interjected and waving my arms into the air.

"I know," Gaby shrieked with excitement.

"I had no idea that I was pregnant! I had no symptoms, still got my period and didn't even *feel* pregnant but I'm very much excited," Gaby boasts. I smiled seeing how happy Gabriela was about bringing a new life into this word despite all the craziness that just happened with her mother popping up and getting shot. It was good to see her in good spirits, so I didn't want to bring up her mother, the shootings or pumpkin right now. It's a time and a place and that place was later.

There was a knock at the door and seconds later, Ricardo entered. He looked so handsome in a pair of black slacks, a navy blue button up shirt and some black Oxford men dress shoes. I ran into his arms, happy to see him after the fucked up shit that I was going through lately. It felt like my life was an emotional rollercoaster ride. I inhaled

the smell of his cologne and immediately felt peace.

"You alright baby," he asked, kissing me on the

forehead.

"Yes, now that you're here." Ricardo glanced

behind me and dropped his arms from around me and

approached his brother and Gaby.

"Hey bro, you good? How are you, Gabriela?"

Ricardo asked with concerned etched on his face and in his

voice.

Ricardo and Paul dapped it up and Ricardo bent

down and kissed Gaby on the cheek. "What are the doctors

saying? Rela told me what happened. I'm sorry that you

had to go through that Gaby."

"She's going to live," Paul said with a slight smile. "She uh—she's also pregnant. Three months to be exact!" Paul said happily.

"What! Congrats bro! I get to have another niece or nephew! I'm all for it. Congrats sis," Ricardo said with genuineness as he hugged his brother.

We sat around kicking it for a bit when I decided to give Paul and Gabriela some time to themselves. She was going to have to be in the hospital for a few days so that they could monitor her. I needed to go and get my son and once I left that's exactly what Ricardo and I did.

Chapter 4

Cadel

It was the last day of vacation and we were definitely enjoying ourselves. A nigga had a tan like no other from being out in the sun, chilling in the pool and lounging on the beach. I definitely skipped on the damn yoga class. You weren't about to see my ass sitting on no mat with my legs crossed, humming with my eyes closed. Hell nah.

Cinnamon was soaking up all the sun and loving the time we've been spending away from home. We had just come back from dinner and I was exhausted and just wanted to sleep before we had to get back on the road in the morning after our checkout.

"Dinner was amazing baby," Cinnamon said as we walked into our hotel room. Cinnamon looked cute in a red asymmetrical cut out Bodycon dress and black stilettos.

She had her hair curled and pinned up. Her body was filling out her dress and I couldn't wait to take it off.

"Yeah, shit was nice. I've enjoyed myself. Let's take a shower together gurl," I said licking my lips as I stared her down hungrily. Cinnamon giggled and tossed her cell phone on the bed.

"Alright, baby daddy. I'll go start the shower." Cinnamon strutted off towards the bathroom.

I made my way towards the bar and popped a bottle of Patron that I'd purchased. I poured a few shots, quickly downing them. The sound of my cell phone ringing caught my attention. I reached inside my denim jean pocket and pulled out my cell phone. It was my cousin Tawny calling.

"What up?" I answered.

"Hey, how's vacation going?"

"It's going good, you know what I'm saying. We out chea. We leave tomorrow, though. How's my son?"

"Zarela came and got him the next day after you dropped him off. I know that you told me not to let her but I don't want to get in the middle of that mess cuz. It ain't cool to keep a parent away from her child."

"Yeah, I feel you. I've been thinking about that too. I've been doing her wrong and it ain't right. I'mma link up with her when I come back to Duval though. Thanks for the heads up cuz."

"No problem. It's all love. Call me if you need me to watch Mayur."

"Will do," I responded and seconds later we hung up.

I think a nigga been spiteful to Rela because of how our relationship ended. Regardless of what has gone down with us, she's a good mother and I could never take our son away from her. The sound of the shower starting caught my attention.

I began to undress when Cinnamon's cell phone began vibrating from off the bed. I walked over and pick up the phone. I sucked my teeth when I saw the name Deon flashing across the screen. What the fuck was up with this nigga? Wait a minute; she was supposed to block this nigga's number in the first place. My blood began to boil when I thought about how Cinnamon had lied to me. I wasted no time answering the phone.

"Who dis?" I barked into the phone.

"Cathy?"

"Nah my nigga, this isn't Cathy. It's her nigga, though. Why you keep calling my chick. What's good?" I was getting heated.

"Yo, put Cathy on the phone and quit playing nigga," Deon yelled back.

"Bruh, I'm not the one. You need to quit calling my chick or there's going to be some serious problems, believe that." I looked up and saw Cinnamon walked out of the bathroom, followed by steam from the shower running.

"What's going on? Why are you yelling," Cinnamon asked as she walked closer to me, in her birthday suit.

"Why this nigga Deon keep calling?" I shouted at Cinnamon as I took the phone slightly away from my ear.

"I don't know," she responded with a dumbass expression on her face.

"What the fuck you mean you don't know? You told me that you were going to block this fuckin' clown. So you lied to me?" I barked. She stood there speechless because she knew that she had been caught. I put the phone back to my ear as I heard Deon still talking shit. I wanted to fuck this nigga up.

"Yo, you don't know?" Deon asked.

"I don't know what?" I held the phone so close to my ear, making sure I wouldn't miss a peep out of what I was about to be told. Cinnamon stood before me butt naked and nervous looking.

"Cinnamon is my baby mama! We share a two-year-old daughter named Milan. So if you excuse me, can you put my stupid ass baby mama on *her* phone please?"

I couldn't believe the bull shit that just came out of this niggas mouth. She had a baby and didn't tell me!? What type of bull shit was she on?

"Really Cinnamon, you have a fuckin' daughter! Mane, talk to your nigga." I tossed the phone towards Cinnamon and she caught it.

I grabbed my jeans, putting them back on and stepping outside on the balcony. I needed a moment. I couldn't believe this bitch would stoop so low as to hide a damn kid from me. She had another thing coming if she thought this shit was about to fly. I stepped back into the hotel room and Cinnamon was going through a screaming match with Deon. I could hear his voice through the phone receiver.

I didn't say shit as I began packing all her shit. If she thought she was gonna still stay with me tonight and ride back to Duval, she had another thing coming. I opened the hotel door and tossed her suitcases into the hallway, scaring a Caucasian man as he briskly walked by with a worried look on his face.

"Cadel—wait what are you doing?" Cinnamon asked as she held the phone away from her ear. I could still hear Deon going off on her about money.

"Get the fuck out!" I barked with veins poking out of the side of my neck and spit flying from my mouth.

"What? Why?" Cinnamon asked with puppy dog eyes and her mouth wide open.

"You're a liar, my nigga. I should've known not to trust a stripper. You're just grimy. Ask your baby father to come and get you because you and I are good. I left my baby mama for you. I was good to your ass and this is how you repay a nigga?" I said with my pointer finger pointing at her as my dreads swung in the air from all the movement I was doing.

"I'm sorry Cadel! I don't have custody of my daughter and Deon does. I pay him child support so telling you about my daughter just wasn't the right time. I didn't know how to tell you either. I'm ashamed!"

"Ashamed? Nah mane, you ain't real. You should've just kept it real. Anybody that would hide they kid whether they have custody or not, can't be trusted about shit else in life," I said making a slash motion under my neck with my hand.

Tears began to fall from my Cinnamon's eyes. I instantly got into a rage seeing her try and play the victim. I grabbed her by her arm and pulled her naked ass towards the front door. I pulled open the front door and pushed her ass right out into the hallway, slamming the door shut.

"Cadel, open up this door! I'm fuckin' naked and I ain't even stripping. Let me get dressed! Open up this door," she barked as she banged on the door.

She could get dressed in the hallway for all I cared. Fuck her!

Chapter 5

Zarela

I was so glad to have my son back with me. He brought such joy into my life. We were having a ball at Pump It Up. I watched as Mayur smiled and giggled as I climbed up one of the bouncy house stairs with him attached to my hip. Once we made it to the top, Mayur sat on my lap and we slid down the slide. All I heard was my son giggling and screaming. He was definitely having a great time.

Once we made it down the slide, Ricardo was standing there and grabbed Mayur from out of my arms. He was so attentive to my son and me. I smiled seeing them running towards another bouncy house. By the time we finished playing for an hour, Mayur was knocked out. Ricardo carried him to the car as my cell phone rang. I watched as Ricardo placed my son into his car seat as I eased my body into my car and stared at my cell phone, surprised to see Cadel calling.

I inhaled and exhaled as I glanced at my cell phone screen. This nigga had some nerve calling me after the bull shit that he has been starting lately. Ricardo eased into the passenger seat of my car as my cell phone continued to ring.

"It's Cadel," I said blowing a raspberry.

"Answer, hear him out and see what he has to say. You two need to come to a resolution and co-parent," Ricardo said with sincerity.

"Fine," I said annoyed because I really didn't want to hear anything Cadel had to say.

"Hello." I rolled my eyes into the back of my head as I answered Cadel's call.

"What's good Rela? How are you?"

"Nothing much. What are you calling for?" I asked getting straight to the point.

"I wanna apologize for all of the bullshit that happened the other day. I ain't fuckin' with Cinnamon no more. She's done. I just wanted to treat you to lunch or something."

I was speechless. Was this Negro trying to come on to me or something?

"Look, I really don't have time for these games," I replied agitatedly. He was starting to annoy me.

"C'mon Rela, please. A nigga won't ask you for shit else if you agree to this."

"Let me think about it and call you back." With that being said, I hung up on his light bright ass.

"What did he say, baby?" Ricardo asked calmly.

"He broke up with ole girl and wants to treat me to lunch or something as an apology. I told him I would get back to him. I don't like the mind games that this man plays."

"I don't know how I feel about that. He has other things on his agenda than just trying to apologize."

"You never know with Cadel." I cranked up my car and backed out of the parking space.

"I don't know what I should do," I confessed.

"Co-parenting doesn't mean lunch outings and dinner dates. I don't think that you should go," Ricardo said feeling slightly bothered.

"Yeah," I replied as I drove us home with a lot on my mind.

~

We arrived at my home and I could tell Ricardo was feeling a certain way because he got really quiet. I was beginning to feel like I should've kept the phone call information to myself if I knew he was going to be upset like this.

"What's wrong? You haven't said much since I mentioned what Cadel said." I flopped down on my bed as Ricardo walked out of the bathroom.

"I'm just not feeling it, baby. Cadel is just going to try and pull you right back into his web." Ricardo sat down next to me on the bed and took off his shoes.

"Well, I kinda want to hear more of what he has to say. I want to be on the same page as him. We have to be civil and cordial with one another for Mayur and if sitting down for lunch or dinner could help, I'm all for it. Besides, I need answers on why he was even thinking or entertaining the idea of trying to go for full custody of our son." Ricardo stood up and began pacing the room. I stared at him confused as to why he was tripping. I stood up and grabbed a bottle of nail polish remover from off of my dresser.

"Look, I love you Rela. I love the foundation that we're building. You were just pregnant with my child," he said sternly as he stared deep into my eyes. I looked down at the floor unable to stare him in the face because I knew the loss of our baby was still hurting him just as much as me. I sat back down on the bed and laid the nail polish remover next to me, not in the mood anymore to remove my nail polish.

"Look at me baby," he said walking over towards me and lifting my chin with his pointer finger causing me to stare him in the face.

"I don't wanna lose you nor have you rethinking *us* for *him*. I know that you're entertaining the idea of going but I ain't feeling it. I gotta put my foot down on this baby.

I forbid you to go." I scrunched up my face as I stared at him, lightly pushing him back as I stood up from off of the bed.

"Forbid me! Ricardo are you crazy? You can't forbid me to not do anything. This is twenty, sixteen man," I said pointing my finger at him.

"Look, if you go and meet with him, I'mma have to chill on us baby girl. There's some shit you just don't do and it's disrespectful to go meet with this clown knowing that I'm feeling a type of way. I would never do something like this to you," Ricardo said crossing his arms across his chest.

"Chill on us? Why are you so threatened? You're saying you would never do anything like this to me but you can't possibly understand because you have no kids or a baby mama!" I yelled.

"I almost had a kid by you," he shot back with hurt imprinted on his face. It was definitely a low blow. I know he was hurt but there was no reason to throw that out there. The pregnancy loss was still very much fresh.

"Look, I'mma ignore that little comment because we're both hurting but whether I have to see him at a restaurant or meet up with him at his house to drop Mayur off, I'm going to still have to see him. He's the father of my son!"

"I'm not trying to hear all that. Dinner and lunch make it too personal. Whatever he gotta tell you, he can tell you over the phone Zarela! Damn. Why aren't you understanding this?" He yelled. I stared at him like he was crazy for yelling at me. This was the first time that he had yelled at me like this and I wasn't feeling his tone.

"You know what? I'm not liking the way that you're talking to me. It's one thing to talk to someone over the phone but it's another when you face to face. I need answers from him. I want him to look at me in my face and apologize. I need that. Please just understand that. I'm not trying to hurt you," I yelled back genuinely.

"Like I said, if you go, I'm good on us. Period!" He barked as he sat down on my bed and began to put his shoes back on.

Yeah, I do agree on something and I think it's best that your ass leave. You're not going to be yelling at me in my own home while my son is sleeping," I said pointing to my bedroom door for him to get the hell out.

"With pleasure! Your behind can't see that I'm trying to look out for you. I'm a guy so I know how other men think. Don't call me when the shit doesn't work out." Ricardo stood up from my bed and walked out without saying another word.

I stood standing in place, not believing what just took place. This man just broke up with me because he *forbids* me to meet with my baby father. I was fuming mad as I grabbed a picture of him and I that was placed in a frame from off my nightstand. I chucked it towards the wall causing the silver frame and glass to shatter. I walked over to my purse that was hanging on my doorknob. I reached inside one of the pockets and grabbed my cell phone.

Walking towards my front door, I stopped to peek inside Mayur's room and to my surprise he was still knocked out and snoring! I guess Pump It Up wore him out. I was glad that the noise and yelling match hadn't waked him. Finally making my way to my front door, I locked it and placed the chain on the latch. Scrolling through my text messages, I settled on Cadel's name. I quickly typed up a text that read, "I'll meet you. Name the time and place."

Ricardo wasn't about to control my moves and since he bailed on me for just initially *entertaining* the idea of going to meet up with Cadel, I was now single and free to do as I please and what I was about to do was meet up with my baby daddy. If Ricardo bailed on me for something this minor, he wasn't the man for me.

Chapter 6

Cadel

I was really pleased that Zarela agreed to meet up with me for dinner. I ain't gonna lie, seeing as how things didn't work out with Cinnamon and me, it made me think about Rela a lot more and made me realize how fucked up a nigga has been treating her. I was foul for a lot of shit that I'd put her through and I just wanted to sincerely apologize to her.

I had stepped out of the shower and wrapped my towel around my waist. I brushed my teeth and walked to my room. I had to make sure I was looking good for Rela. I'm feeling like I want that old thing back, but that's not why I invited her out. A nigga truthfully wanted to apologize to her.

After drying off, I walked into my closet and pulled off a hanger that held a pair of dark denim jeans. I decided to pair my jeans with a black shirt that had the words "NWA" in bold white lettering. I tossed the clothes on my bed and began putting on some smell good. I glanced at the clock and noticed that time was ticking away and I needed to get a move on if I was going to be on time for this dinner date with Rela.

After putting on my clothes, I placed my herringbone chain around my neck and put on my Michael Kors Champagne men's watch. I was looking fresh to death so it was only right to pair the fit with a clean ass pair of Jay's. Once I took a quick look at myself in the mirror, I was satisfied with how I was rolling. I placed my gold grill in my mouth, grabbed my cell phone, wallet and keys and was out the door.

Pulling up to Wasabi, I sent Rela a quick text message letting her know that I was here. I was praying that she hadn't arrived yet and maybe was on CP time. To my surprise, she texted me back that she was just pulling up as well. I smiled that she was meeting with me considering all the bull shit that took place lately.

I stepped out of my car and made the way to the front entrance of the restaurant. I stood waiting patiently for Rela to walk up. When I glanced down the sidewalk I saw her walking towards me and my God she was looking good. Her hair was out in its natural state, all curly and healthy. She was rocking a white short-sleeve, knee-length floral dress that fit her body like a glove. I admired how tight the dress was. She was definitely working it. I licked my lips and rubbed my hands together as I admired her beauty. I could see those pretty ass feet in some red strappy sandals. I smiled not even realizing it. She was definitely doing it for me.

"Hey beautiful, thanks for meeting me," I said kissing her on the cheek.

"No problem," she replied, not smiling and being cold towards me. I knew she was still upset for some of the shit that went down between us, mainly the gas station brawl. I was going to fix that, though.

"You look amazing, you know that," I said holding open the entrance front door.

"Thank you," she said walking inside, still not cracking a smile. I shook my head and smirked at how tough she was acting. We approached the greeter and were immediately sat down at a secluded table. The greeter passed us some menus and informed us that someone would come by to take our orders shortly.

"So, let me just start off by thanking you for meeting me. I know you didn't have to but I'm really glad that you did."

"Yeah, well meeting with you made me lose my man, so this better be good," she interjected as she scanned the menu and then looked back up at me. Just staring at her

in those beautiful eyes had a nigga blushing.

"Oh, word? Ya man's left you over a little dinner

date with your baby daddy?" I asked as if I didn't hear her

clearly the first time. I chuckled at how threatened her

nigga was.

"Yeah, he did. He wasn't feeling this and felt like

he could control me by forbidding me not to come." Zarela

shook her head.

"Damn. Well, I'm sorry. I ain't mean to cause no

trouble. How's my son?" I asked changing the subject.

"He's fine. I didn't like that shit you pulled at the

gas station. Why were you trying to go for full custody

Cadel? Really? I am not a bad mother! You know that I'm

not," she said with anger as she slammed her fist down on

the table.

"I know that. I'm sorry. Just let me explain why."
Before I could explain, a waiter approached our table.

"Are you two ready to order?"

"Uh—lemme get uh—the house fried rice, the lobster and dynamite roll. Let me also get the Tequila Sunrise drink please," I said to the waiter. I closed my menu and handed it to him.

"No problem sir, and for you?" The waiter asked, staring at me.

"I'll take the California roll, shrimp teriyaki and a Zombie as my drink."

"I'll put these orders in right away." The waiter grabbed Zarela's menu and walked off.

"As I was saying, I was mad as hell how you left me once I was in jail and moved on with ole boy. I felt like I did all this changing for you and made myself a better man for you and my son and one little incident and you bailed. That shit hurt Rela. I changed for you, you left, I was good to Cinnamon and she did me dirty. I was childish as fuck for thinking I would go for sole custody. You're a wonderful mother to Mayur."

Zarela sat there with glossy eyes as she grabbed a napkin and dabbed her eyes. "Thank you for that apology. I really needed to hear that. I'm a damn good mother and that shit hurt me to the core to hear those words from Cinnamon's mouth." At that moment, the waiter came back with our alcoholic drinks.

"Let's make a toast," I asked raising my glass.

"A toast to what?" Rela asked eyeing me suspiciously but still raising up her glass as well.

"A toast to being better and moving on," I said as we clanked our glasses together.

"So, I remember you saying that you and ole ugly was no more. What happened?" I laughed at how Rela was taking shots at Cinnamon.

"Well, I found out the broad had a child behind my back! She has a two-year-old that she doesn't have custody of. The nigga kept calling and she blew it off a couple of times, making it seem like it was somebody from the past that she don't fuck with any more. She promised to block his number but didn't. When she was in the shower and I saw the nigga calling again, I answered and he told me everything that I needed to know."

"Wow! That's fuckin' crazy Cadel!" Zarela said in amazement. She picked up her drink and sipped from it.

"You telling me. There's more, the bitch stole from me! I guess she did it while I stepped out on the balcony to get some fresh air when I called her out on her shit. She took like three hundred from out of my wallet! I'mma pay her fuckin' ass a visit at the strip club too. The bitch wanna steal from me!" I shook my head just thinking about the foul shit Cinnamon did. Her little hoe ass was about to get a visit from me real soon.

"Oh my, goodness Cadel! This is what happens when you date a stripper who calls everybody baby daddy. She's so stupid," Rela said shaking her head.

"You're right. The whole situation with her having a kid got me thinking how I turned my back on my own kid with Pumpkin. I need to step up and take responsibility for the kid that's mine."

"Wow, that's really big of you to say. I really like hearing this," she said placing her glass down.

The waiter walked up with our plates and gently sat them down on the table. "Enjoy. Is there anything else you need?"

"Nah, we're good. Thank you," I responded. The waiter trotted off and I put my attention back on Rela.

"I think a nigga was just in denial that I had another kid and it was by someone that wasn't you. It felt like time a nigga got himself together, life was throwing me all kinds of curve balls. First, the baby shit with Pumpkin, then the bull shit with Paul, then jail and then Pumpkin dying and you and I breaking up, shit hit me hard and all at once," I said taking a bite out of my food.

"This is very big of you to admit. Shit are you sure that you're the same Cadel that used to be my unfaithful baby daddy?" Rela joked.

"Yo," I laughed. "I hated and still hate when you call me that ugly shit," I chuckled.

"So what's been up with you?" I asked wiping my hands on a napkin.

"What's not been happening? So—well—I was pregnant but—I lost the baby."

I sat up upon hearing that she was pregnant. I hated thinking about that nigga all up in them guts and busting in her. Shit, I was her first and only until that nigga came along.

"Damn. I'm sorry to hear that," I said sincerely trying to downplay my anger that she was pregnant. I didn't think the shit between them was that serious.

"Thank you. I'm dealing with it. It's hard especially because Gabriela is pregnant. She's three months and didn't even know it until she got shot."

"Shot? Who the fuck shot her? Not gangsta Gabriela! All jokes aside, she good?"

"Yeah, she was hit in the shoulder after her crazy ass mama appeared after being released from prison with her sister. We found out that Pumpkin and Gabriela were related. They had the same mother but different father. Paul showed up and all hell broke loose when Gabriela was shot and her mother's sister was killed. I thought I was going to die," she said sadly, losing her appetite since she pushed her food away and grabbed another napkin. She couldn't stop the silent tears from falling.

I couldn't believe the bullshit that I was hearing about Gaby and Pumpkin being related. So much information was coming my way from Zarela that I couldn't keep up. Shit was definitely crazy. I got up from my seat across from her and sat next to her, wrapping my arm around her neck and pulling her into me. "I thought I wasn't going to see Mayur again," she cried. The waiter approached us and I kindly asked for some boxes and the check.

"Look, let's get out of here. I don't want you crying up in here. I know that shit was scary for you but you're alive and well. Don't stress on what could've been, focus on the present." She sat up and wiped away her tears. She sniffled a bit before she reached into her purse and pulled out a compact mirror.

"You're still beautiful."

"Boy quit it!" She said lightly shoving me. "After all this crying, I'm trying to make sure that I don't have a booger in my nose," she joked, putting her mirror away. I couldn't do anything but laugh.

I paid the bill as we scraped our food into our takeout boxes. We walked outside, side by side as we stood in front of the restaurant building. The night's air felt hot and clammy. The sound of bugs chirping and cars passing by was all that could be heard since neither one of us said anything.

"Soo—thanks for the food and the apology. I needed to hear that."

"No problem. God put that on my heart to apologize to you. My karma was Cinnamon. Anyway, where's your car? I would love to walk you safely to it," I asked licking my lips.

"It's right there," she pointed a few feet away. "I think I can manage," she said winking.

"Alright," I said smiling. "Well, can I have a hug?" Zarela stood before me looking me up and down as she smirked.

"I guess," she said, smiling.

I wrapped my arms around her waist as she leaned into me, hugging me back. She smelled heavenly. I didn't want to let her go. I kissed her on the cheek and watched her walk away to her car. At that moment, I knew I needed to get my family back. There wasn't shit else in this world for me.

Chapter 7

Zarela

Once I made it safely to my car, I had to catch my breath. I couldn't believe that Cadel had apologized to me. It seemed like he was really trying to turn over a new leaf. I watched him in my rearview mirror walk away in the opposite direction from me to his car. It was something about the way that he was at dinner that intrigued my interest in him. I quickly shook the thoughts of me considering giving Cadel another chance out of my head.

I decided to give Ricardo a call to let him know how the dinner date went. I figured maybe he had time to cool down and to see how much he overreacted yesterday. The phone rang for a few seconds until his voicemail picked up. I took the phone away from my ear and glanced at it, surprised that he was still mad and tripping. I hung up, deciding not to leave a message. He was seriously bugging out. He always encouraged us to get along and to co-parent but yet he gets offended by a little dinner date with my son's father. What kind of shit was that? Am I wrong? I don't think that I am. We kept everything cordial and respectful between us. I wish that Ricardo could see that.

I cranked up my car and made my way home. I had a little bit of wine left in the fridge and a bubble bath was calling my name. I called Gaby while I sat at a red light to check up on her and update her on what was going on with me. I hastily scrolled for her number before the light turned green. Gabriela answered on the third ring.

"Hey, best friend," I sang into the phone. "How are you?"

"Hey boo, I'm doing okay considering everything that's been going on." Gabriela and I haven't spoken much about what went down at her house and I was afraid to bring it up. I didn't want to say anything unless she chooses to.

"How are you feeling?"

"I'm alright, I still don't feel pregnant. It's crazy to believe there's a life growing inside of me and I didn't even know," she said with excitement.

"I'm so happy for you," I said genuinely.

"Thank you. It's crazy that somehow after all the shitty things that happened, I was blessed with this pregnancy. My mother has always tried so hard to ruin me and my life and I still came out on top. I hope she rots in prison. It's unfortunate that Pumpkin and I didn't know that we were related until after her death." My skin instantly covered in Goosebumps when Gabriela brought up Pumpkin's death.

"I still can't believe that happened. Have the police said anything about the investigation?" I said hitting the gas and driving home.

"Yessssss," she dragged out. "I meant to update you on everything. They found out that the brake line to the car Pumpkin was driving was rigged. It had my mother's fingerprints on it. You know she used to be a mechanic back in the day. With the murder of Pumpkin, her dude and then Isadora sister getting killed because of her, she won't be seeing the light of day."

"Wow, I'm speechless. I can't believe she would do something like that," I said shaking my head.

"I can because I grew up with her. I haven't told the boys yet about her popping up. I don't think I am. I just want to celebrate this new life I'm creating and my wedding. Once the wedding is over, we're going to start looking for a house. I can't stay here knowing that someone was killed in my home and that I was shot by my mother. I don't want that kind of energy. Right now I just want to focus on the positive. I don't want to give my mother any more energy than I already have," she said firmly.

I was so proud of how well Gabriela was taking everything that had been thrown at her. She was so strong and I was pleased to call her my best friend. She has been through so much and still manages to come out strong and on top.

"I totally feel you. That's the spirit. I think moving would be best too. I'm so proud of how positive you're being. Well, my dinner date went well with Cadel. Of course, you know that Negro Ricardo is mad that I went and meet Cadel so he broke up with me but I'm glad that I went. Cadel has turned over a new leaf." I went on to explain to Gabriela about the conversation he and I had. I turned down on my street and pulled into my apartment complex and was in the middle of talking when I noticed Cadel's truck parked a few feet away.

"Girl, let me call you back. I just pulled up to my place and Cadel is here. I told him that Mayur was with his grandpa tonight, so I don't know why he's over here."

"Girl, I hope he's not trying to start any shit. Call me back later or better yet, just text me," Gaby said as we ended our call.

I cut off my car, grabbed my purse, my cell phone and got out. I slowly walked towards my apartment building stairs. I was hoping that this Negro wasn't about to start no mess after the good dinner date that we just had. I was also confused on what he was doing at my place. Little by little I walked up the stairs to my apartment, upon reaching the top step, I see Cadel leaning against my apartment door holding a bouquet of red roses.

"Cadel, what are you doing here?" I asked slowly walking towards him as he extended the flowers towards me. I gently grabbed them and sniffed them. They smelled lovely.

"I wanna talk to you," he said.

"Thank you so much for the flowers. What do you want to talk about?" I asked unlocking my front door.

"May I come in?" He asked patiently as he stood in the hallway.

"I guess," I said shrugging my shoulders.

I walked into the kitchen rummaging through my cabinets to find a vase to place my roses in. I felt Cadel standing behind me so I grabbed a vase and turned around. He was standing behind me just staring at me.

"What are you looking at?" I asked confusingly with a weird smirk on my face. I placed my roses into the vase and began adding water.

"Matter of fact, what are these roses for?"

"Zarela, I want that old thing back. I want my family. There ain't shit out there for me. I changed for you and gave all my love to the wrong woman who in return did me wrong. Meeting up with you earlier really had a nigga feeling good," he confessed. I stood staring at him as I leaned back on the counter and crossed my arms across my chest. I was blown away by him wanting to get back with me.

"I—I don't know what to say Cadel. We've tried to make it work, lots of times. I don't –I don't know," I stuttered. I kicked my heels off and looked back at him.

Cadel walked closer to me and invaded my personal space. My heart began to race. He was so close to me that I could smell his breath. He looked damn good though with those dreads hanging down and that gold grill sitting in the bottom row of his teeth.

"Cadel, we can't," I muttered as he stood in front of me, placing both his arms side by side, pinning me in place.

He leaned into me and began planting delicate long kisses on my neck. It felt so good but I couldn't go down this route with him. I gently tried to move my neck from side to side as I tried to push him away from me but it was no use. He had me locked in like a Venus flytrap. He placed his hands on each knee and slid them under my dress, slowly rising it up as he kept his hands on my thighs.

"Cadel, I can't go there with you anymore," I whispered with my eyes closed as he had my dress lifted over my ass.

"You know that you still love me, though," he said pushing my panties to the side and caressing my second set of lips with his fingers. My juices immediately coated his fingers. My breathing became labored. Cadel lifted me onto the counter and pulled down my panties, pulling them off and tossing them to the floor. My mind was telling me to stop him but it was something about him that kept pulling me back.

Cadel's mouth found his way to my kitty. A whimper escaped my mouth and I bit my bottom lip. He took his tongue and lapped up my pussy as if he was a dog drinking from his bowl. I began grinding on his face as he continued to run his tongue in circles on my kitty. He inserted a finger inside of me as he continued to gobble up my juices like it was Thanksgiving Day.

"Cadel," I whimpered as I pulled on his dreads.

"You like that shit girl, I can tell by how you're coming in my mouth," Cadel boasted as he came up for air. I opened my eyes seeing my juices glistening on his mouth.

He licked his lips and went back down on me. My eyes rolled into the back of my head.

"God, I'm coming," I shouted.

Cadel wasted no time as he vacuumed all of my juices out of my pussy. I was panting and out of breath but Cadel wasted no time as he unbuttoned his jeans and pulled them down. He gently lifted me off of the counter and turned me around, leaning me on the counter. Before I could even brace myself, Cadel slid inside of me in one swift and quick motion. I held onto the counter with all my might as he began to give me deep, hard strokes.

"Yesssss," I hissed as Cadel continued to hit it from the back. I threw it back trying to match him but he was giving it to me so good that I couldn't move. I just closed my eyes and enjoyed the D that Cadel was serving.

"I love you," I yelled out.

"I love you too gurl, I never stopped," he said in between grunts as he pulled out and slide back in repeatedly.

"Stopppp teasing meeeee," I said in between moans. Cadel then placed his left hand on the back of my neck and he continued to stroke me and not too long after those strokes, I creamed all over him as my warm liquid trickled down my leg. Cadel pulled out as he shot the rest of his babies on my ass.

I giggled as I grabbed a paper towel and wiped myself clean. I grabbed another paper towel, turned on my faucet and lightly wet the paper towel, passing it to Cadel so he could wipe himself off. The sound of my doorbell made me jump.

"You expecting someone gurl," Cadel asked as he pulled his jeans up and walked into the living room.

"I wasn't expecting anyone, not even you," I joked. I jogged towards my front door and peeked through my peephole and was shocked to see Ricardo standing on the other side.

"What the hell," I mumbled. I quickly pulled down my dress and slowly opened the door, partially standing behind it.

"Hey," Ricardo said with a slight smile on his face.

"What's up?" I asked surprisingly but didn't bother to return a smile to him. I didn't appreciate him breaking up with me and ignoring me when I still tried to reach out to him after I left the restaurant. Yet he felt it was okay to bring his ass to my crib after he dismissed me.

"Well, may I come in? I wanna talk to you," he asked, trying to look behind me to see what I wouldn't invite him in.

"I have company right now."

"Oh wow, really Zarela? This is how you do?" Ricardo asked with hurt on his face.

"Ayyy Rel, you alright baby," Cadel asked from behind me but out of Ricardo's view.

"Wow, that voice sounds familiar," Ricardo said sarcastically, rubbing his chin.

"Look, you broke up with me and I'm single. Cadel is my baby father. What do you expect?" I asked stepping from behind the door and opening it slightly wider.

Ricardo's eyes turned big like saucers as he saw Cadel behind me. I turned around and saw that Cadel didn't have his denim jeans buttoned or zipped up. Just looking at him anyone would know that we just fucked.

"I came over here to apologize and to try and make things right yet you fuckin' your ex. A man that's constantly dogged you out and cheats on you. I've been

nothing but good to you and this is what your ass do!"

Ricardo shouted.

"Stop yelling in my building and tone your voice

down!"

"Nah, fuck that! Don't call me when that man

breaks your heart," Ricardo sternly said.

Before I could even react or reply, Cadel flew out of

the front door, brushing past me as he charged at Ricardo.

Cadel threw a left and right punch to Ricardo's face

causing him to fly to the ground. Cadel started tagging his

ass and Ricardo couldn't keep up as he grabbed a hold of

Cadel's dreads.

"My nigga you pulling hair like a bitch! Let my shit

go and I'll let you up and we can square up fair and

square," Cadel roared.

Ricardo let go of his dreads and Cadel stood back, letting Ricardo get up. They squared up and Ricardo threw a left, Cadel ducked and wrapped his arms around Ricardo, trying to body slam him. They tussled for a bit and Cadel let him go, hitting him with another right and left, he threw in a couple body shots to Ricardo's upper torso.

"Stop! Please, stop this shit," I yelled as I tried to break them up, only Cadel pushed me back, causing me to stumble.

"Get back Rela," Cadel shouted.

Ricardo finally hit Cadel square in the jaw. The two continued to go back and forth, blow for blow. Blood flew from Ricardo's mouth when Cadel hit him in the mouth, causing his top lip to split.

"Oh my God, quit it," I cried out!

They were out for blood and there was no way that I could stop them. Cadel was putting in work on Ricardo but Ricardo was still giving Cadel a run for his money but from looking at Ricardo's face, he would for sure need an icepack.

"Oh my God," I shouted, frazzled.

I ran back into my house and filled up a pot of cold water. I anxiously waited for it to fill to the top. Once it was filled, I picked up the pot and walked as fast as I could outside without spilling any water. I made it outside in my hallway and Cadel and Ricardo was still going for another round.

"You bitch ass nigga, trying to come between me and my babymama. That's always gonna be my pussy, my nigga," Cadel roared.

"Stop!" I shouted! They ignored me. Cadel grabbed Ricardo from around the waist and slammed him on the pavement!

"BAM!"

"Oh my, God," I yelled. Ricardo was fucked up, yet he still got up trying to fight back. I had seen enough and tossed the cold pot of water on them, causing them to stop fighting. I grabbed Cadel by his wrist and pulled him with all my might into my house, closing the door behind him.

I ran towards Ricardo who looked like a monster. His lip was split, he had a knot the size of a golf ball on his forehead and his nose was leaking. I tried to grab him to see how serious his injuries were but he forcefully pushed me away.

"Don't touch me. I'm good. I hope that man breaks your heart and steps on it repeatedly. I've been nothing but a good man to you. I can't believe that you would try me like this. Have a nice life. Don't call me when you regret your decision." Ricardo walked off, leaving a trail of blood as he descended down the stairs without another word.

I stood there trying to catch my breath and get myself together. I couldn't believe the shit that just went down. I never wanted Cadel or Ricardo to get hurt or cause chaos like this. I exhaled and walked back into my house. Cadel was in my bedroom, tying up his dreads. He had a small cut under his eye but other than that, you couldn't tell that he was just in a brawl.

"That nigga asked for that shit Rel, I've let that nigga talk and talk."

I walked up to him and grabbed his face. "I hate that that shit went down like that. Why'd you have to do that? You should've let me handle everything." Cadel lightly snatched his face from my grasped.

"Nah, I handled the shit. I changed a lot for you and I didn't like the way that he was talking to you with him raising his voice at you like that. The shit ain't up for debate Zarela. The nigga dipped on you for meeting up with your baby father, the fuck type of shit he on? If you love someone you don't dip out that easily," he said starting me in the eyes.

I blew air out of my lips, he had a point.

"Well, are you okay?"

"Yo, I'm good gurl. I promise you that," he said grabbing me by my face and kissing me on the lips. The kiss lasted for at least a minute as our tongues danced with each other. It felt so right kissing him that I didn't want the kiss to stop.

"I'm staying here tonight. You are my woman. I belong with my family. I changed for you and gave all my love and respect to the wrong woman who in return fucked me over. That ain't nothing but God and Karma. I'm sorry for the pain that I caused you but a nigga doesn't want to be an *unfaithful baby daddy*, as you call me. I wanna be a man to you. Let me be that and prove to you Zarela," he said staring me sincerely in my eyes.

Tears began to fall from my eyes as I heard Cadel confess this to me. What was strange was that I actually believed him. I wrapped my arms around his neck and buried my head into his neck.

"I love you Zarela."

"I love you too Cadel. I just can't seem to shake you."

"It's because you love me. You can't run from true love. Now let's go take a shower together because daddy's home," Cadel said walking off towards the bathroom.

Chapter 8

Cadel

It's been about a week since Rela and I decided to try and make this thing work between us again. I promised her that I would do right and nothing or no bitch would knock me off my square again. I decided to meet up with the case worker who called me about Pumpkins kids. I had been doing a lot of thinking and I was wrong for how I acted when I found out that I had another kid. Those babies didn't ask to be born. I rolled over and pulled Zarela closer to me. She shifted in her sleep and moaned. Within a few seconds, she turned around and opened her eyes, smiling at me.

"Good morning," she whispered.

"Good morning beautiful. You want some breakfast?"

"I could go for some of that," she said yawning.

"Damn gurl, cover that mouth," I joked, scrunching up my face.

"Boy you crazy, your breath is kicking too," she said lightly pushing me.

"I'm just kidding gurl, let me get up and start this breakfast because I have to go and meet the case worker for the kid."

I got out of bed, stretched and brushed my teeth. I took a quick shower and got dressed. Once I was finished, I went and started on breakfast. I fumbled through the cabinets for the right pots and pans and began getting to work. I whipped up some green bell pepper and onion omelets with cheese and crispy bacon. I poured her a glass of orange juice.

"Babe, here you go, you better eat this while it's hot."

Zarela sat up in bed as I handed her the hot plate. "Thank you, babe, it looks so good." She said a quick prayer over her food and began digging in.

"I hope that you enjoy your breakfast because I have to run. I'll call you once I leave the case worker and let you know what's up with everything."

"Okay babe," Zarela said with a mouth full of food.

I rushed out the door. I was nervous as hell meeting up with this case worker, though.

~

I first made a pit stop to Wal-Mart. I couldn't leave with my daughter until I had a car seat. I rushed through the packed Wal-Mart and made my way to the baby section. I grabbed a Graco car seat for one hundred dollars and some odds and ends like Good Start formula, diapers and wipes. I then proceeded to checkout. While standing in line, I glanced over and saw Cinnamon's trifling ass. She was in line with some green ass looking nigga, spending his money. She didn't see me. I wanted nothing more than to confront her ass about the few hundred that she stole from me but I needed to stay focused. I would handle her hoe ass later.

Once I left Wal-mart, drama free, I drove for twenty minutes. I arrived at Child Protective Services. A nigga was actually nervous. Each step I walked, it felt like my heart starting beating faster and faster. I walked inside the dull building and was greeted by a receptionist.

"Um—I'm here to see Rosie," I rattled off to the woman as I glanced around the room.   "Name?" She asked bleakly.

"Cadel Wright," I answered. The receptionist didn't respond, she only typed into her computer, I guess searching for my name.

"You may have a seat and she will be with your shortly."

I didn't respond as I just walked off and made my way to an empty black vinyl seat. I quickly sent Rela a text letting her know that I had made it. A few seconds went by before she responded and told me to keep her posted. Before I knew it more people were piling into the building. The more I noticed other people's names that came in after me were being called and being seen, it started to make me mad. I stood up and walked backed over to the nonchalant receptionist who now appeared to be frazzled.

"Excuse me, mam, I've been waiting for almost an hour. When will I be seen?"

"Sir, you have to wait your turn like everyone else," she answered, not even bothering to give me any eye contact.

"I have been waiting my turn but you got other folk coming in here after me yet being seen before me. What's up with that?"

"Have a seat before I have security called over," she responded with annoyance, this time finally glancing up at me. All I noticed were her yellow ass teeth.

"Man, that ain't even necessary. You need to call a damn dentist for them yellow ass teeth," I mumbled, turning around and walking off back over to my seat, to find out that it now had been occupied. I stood up, posted against the wall as I tried to calm myself down. I felt my fuse getting short.

"Mr. Wright, Cadel Wright," a short attractive Puerto Rican woman called.

I was silently happy that my name was now called because after dealing with the rude ass receptionist, bad ass kids running around and babies crying, I was about to lose my cool and just walk out. I quickly walked over to the woman, I assumed to be my caseworker. She extended her hand with a smile on her face.

"Hi, I'm Rosie Marisol, nice to meet you, Mr. Wright." I shook her hand and returned the smile.

"Likewise."

"I'm so glad that you could come in today. Please, follow me."

I followed her down a hallway with off-white walls and scuffed up linoleum tile floors. I passed by different rooms with different caseworkers and families. Finally, we stopped at an unoccupied room. The room wasn't all that big. It was nothing special about it either. There were a few cartoon characters on the bright yellow wallpaper. I glanced at her messy desk that bejeweled baby pictures, I'm assuming to be her kid. Behind her desk sat a huge black file cabinet.

"Please, have a seat," she offered as she closed the door to the room. I sat down and crossed my arms across my chest. It was hot as fuck in this room or maybe I was just nervous.

"So, I'm really glad to have you in my office today. As you know, Patricia or Pumpkin, as many knew her by was killed with her husband. You two had a relationship or relations. As you also know, you agreed to take a DNA test. I have the results here. We ordered another duplicate copy straight from the testing agency." She passed me the test results. I read the results word for word.

"Cadel Wright is excluded as the biological father of Courtney Wright. The Combined Paternity Index is 0 and the Probability of Paternity is 0%. Cadel Wright is not excluded as the biological father of Cassandra Wright. The Combined Paternity Index is 100 or larger and the Probability of Paternity is 99.999% or higher." I wiped my face trying to get rid of the sweat. Having another kid kind of scared a nigga but in a way, I was up for the challenge.

"Wow, so where do we go from here?" I asked placing the paper down on her desk.

"We have Cassandra here. Are you ready to meet her?"

"Yeah—yes, I'm ready," I said wiping my palms on my denim jeans.

"It'll just be one second. Excuse me," she said with a smile as she exited the room. I took a deep breath and began tapping my foot. Within a few minutes, Rosie returned with the cutest little girl ever in her arms.

"Cadel, meet your daughter Cassandra. She's three months," she said smiling as I stood up. She passed her to me and I held her in my arms, smiling at how beautiful she was. I lightly grabbed her hand and to my surprise, she wrapped her tiny little finger around one of my fingers. I stroked her little head which was full of curly black strands of hair. She was golden as the sun with her light skin. Her beautiful brown eyes glistened as she stared back at me with drool running from her mouth. She smiled a toothless grin as I began speaking to her. In plain words, she immediately melted my heart.

"Hi Cassandra, it's your daddy baby girl. Forgive daddy for being away for so long. I was an idiot," I said as sweetly as my masculine and deep voice would allow. Cassandra continued to smile at me as if she understood every word that I was saying.

"Well, I hate to interrupt this precious moment, but we have some paperwork to fill out and you and Cassandra can be on your way." Rosie grabbed my daughter from my arms and I began filling out the necessary documents so that I could take my daughter home. The more I began signing my name, the more I thought about Courtney.

"Um—look, I know that I'm not the father of her twin sister, but I can't fathom how my daughter would feel growing up knowing that she had a sister out there. I can't believe that I'm saying this," I paused and chuckled lightly. "Is there any way that I could gain custody of Courtney as well? I don't want her growing up in foster care. I've heard horrible stories. I want to do the right thing," I said looking into Rosie's eyes.

"Wow, Mr. Wright, I'm surprised and shocked, but in a good way. You're a standup man. When we first talked on the phone, you were the complete opposite in my opinion. I think you were initially just scared but you've come around and accepted what is what. I'd be happy to start the process of adopting Courtney for you. Now you won't be able to take her home today, but if all goes well and checks out, there shouldn't be a problem," she said standing up from her desk. I slid the papers across her desk and reached for Cassandra who was falling asleep. She was precious.

"Thank you so much. I guess we will be going," I said shaking Rosie's hand.

"We will be in touch. Have a great day," she said seeing me out the door.

I walked to my car as the sun shined down on me. It felt like it was God telling me that I did the right thing as a father and as a man. I couldn't wait for Zarela to meet Cassandra.

Chapter 9

Cadel

I pulled up to Zarela's apartment and hopped out of my truck. I grabbed a still sleeping Cassandra out of her car seat and my Wal-Mart bags. I walked up the steps and knocked on Rela's door. I thought to myself that a nigga was gonna need a key because there was no way that I was going to be knocking like this. Within a few seconds, my beautiful baby girl Rela answered.

"Oh my goodness," she squealed, stepping to the side to let us enter.

"Isn't she cute," I added with a smile. My daughter was already giving me a soft spot.

"She really is! May I hold her?"

"Of course!" I passed Cassandra to Rela and sat down my Wal-Mart bags.

"I see you went shopping daddy daycare," she joked.

"Well you know, I had to get my princess right," I smirked as I took a seat on the sofa. Zarela sat down next to me as Cassandra woke up, mean mugging us. Her facial expressions were too funny.

"Hi pretty girl," Rela softly said in the cutest baby voice.

"Bwawaaawaaaa," Cassandra cooed as if she was trying to tell us something. We giggled at how much she was talking. I instantly felt bad on missing out on her first three months of life but I made a promise to myself that I was going to be in her life from here on out.

"So—I was talking to my case worker and I was thinking that I would take custody of Courtney, the other twin. A nigga couldn't live with himself for splitting two sisters up, twins at that."

There was a slight pause before Zarela glanced at me. "I think that's the most upstanding and mature thing that you've said in a long time," she leaned over and pursed her lips together. I leaned into her and placed my lips on hers. We began to share a passionate kiss.

"What time is my main man coming home?"

"Mayur will be here before dinner. My dad called and said that they were out at the zoo for the day."

"My son knows he stays on the move," I said shaking my head and laughing at how Mayur was always on the go.

"Is this hard for you?" I asked changing the subject to something more serious.

"Hard for me?" Zarela asked confusingly.

"Being around a baby and possibly another one?"

She looked down at Cassandra who was trying to look around but hadn't quite mastered fully holding her head up yet.

"I'm not going to lie, I'm a little sad that my best friend is now pregnant and there will be two new babies into our home but I'll be okay. Matter of fact, I was thinking about how Isadora claimed Gabriela and Pumpkin were sisters so in a way, Cassandra is Gaby's niece. Isn't that something?"

"Damn, that shit is crazy. I hadn't thought about it. Sounds like some Maury plot twist shit," I laughed. I slowly straightened my face and stared at Zarela.

"You know I'mma put another baby in you and give you my last name girl. No bull shit but God knew you weren't supposed to have a baby with the shady clown ass nigga which is why things didn't work out with the pregnancy. Mark my words. You're gonna be big and fat soon!" Zarela laughed and lightly pushed me with her right hand while still holding Cassandra securely with her left hand.

"Well, if you don't mind watching Cassandra, I gotta make a quick run right quick." I stood up and stretched. Zarela gave me the most annoyed look.

"Mane, Rela don't be eyeing me like that. I'm not on no hoe shit. I swear. I just need to go and take care of something. I'll be back. I promise."

"Alright," she said with a slight attitude. I knew she didn't quite trust me and knew that I was going to have to regain her trust. I was willing to work for it because I loved her that much.

"Look, to put your mind at ease, I'm meeting up with my boys for some drinks at the strip. I need to check Cinnamon for stealing from me. If she thought she was gonna get away with that fuck shit, she had another thing coming."

Zarela scrunched up her face and twisted up her lips as she stood up and placed Cassandra in Mayur's old baby swing that she had set up. "Let that shit go. You aren't hurting from that loss. Let her crab ass have it. That's all she knows is how to be is shady."

"I hear you but I'm a man and I can't let anybody disrespect me, you feel me? I swear I'mma be good. I'm coming home to you and only you. I'll even call you when I get there, text you while I'm there and call you when I leave. Does that make you feel better?" I asked walking up to her and wrapping my arms around her waist. She pouted and crossed her arms while avoiding eye contact with me.

"Rela, baby, I know I hurt you but I promise I won't ever hurt you again. You feel me?" She stared at the floor, still pouting and ignoring me.

"You feel me?" I asked again, lightly tickling her. She began to smile as she tried to squirm away. I grabbed her face and brought her lips to mine.

"I love you, I'll be back."

"I love you too," she said watching me walk out the door and locking it behind me.

I've got to get my key back!

~

I made my way into the strip club searching for my boys. It had been a minute since we met up. I saw my niggas at the bar and rolled up on them. They were chilling at the bar, passing a blunt around.

"What up fools?" I asked smirking as I sat down.

My boys consisted of my nigga, Boobie, who wasn't anything to mess with, Big Man, who was just like his nickname, big as hell. He looked like Rick Ross before the weight loss. Last, but not least, my nigga Lil Step, who was short as fuck. These three niggas were my A 1's, and if I had a problem with somebody, they all did. We were thick as thieves and tighter than a strippers drawls.

"What ya'll boys drinkin' on?" I asked loudly over the blaring music.

"Crown and coke," they all said in unison.

"I should've known," I laughed. That was the only shit we preferred to drink. I slapped my hand on the bar a few times as I yelled for the bartender's attention. Finally getting little mama's notice, she sashayed over.

"Crown and coke please," I sat down a twenty dollar bill. The bartender quickly made my drink, took my money and sat down my cup of liquor. She then moved on to the next customer.

"Y'all see that thieving ass Cinnamon round here?" I scanned the dimly lit club.

"Nah, I ain't seen her," Lil Step slurred. "If I had, she would be putting this D in her mouth!" We all fell out laughing. My nigga Step was already fucked up. I downed my drink as Yung Thug, "Thief in the Night," featuring Trouble blasted.

"So, what's going on with the trap?" Big Man asked.

A lot of motherfucka's didn't know that I ran a trap. I kept that shit tip top secret. It was run by my boys and me. We weren't deep in the game but we did supply some of the best cocaine, pills and weed. We made good off the shit too. Big Man, Boobie and Lil Step ran the shit. I never got my hands dirty. All them nigga's knew how to do was get money out in the streets.

Big Man didn't finish the eighth grade; Boobie became acquainted with the streets when he was seventeen after he found his mother and father in his living room dead from an overdose. Lil Step had tons of kids and decided the best way to keep his wages from being garnished for child support was to get tax free money in the streets. My boys were crazy as fuck but that was just who they were. I didn't want to do this shit forever which was why I just controlled the trap. I supplied what we needed, checked on the trap and collected my money.

"Everything is good boss. We got shit under control," Lil Step slurred.

"Nigga shut up with your drunk ass," Big Man laughed. I swear every time this nigga laughed it sounded like thunder. His voice was so damn deep that it was scary to a person who didn't know him. Before we could finish our conversation, the DJ interrupted us.

"Alright nah, we got a club favorite about to grace the stage. Y'all get your tens, twenties and hundreds ready, hell even one and five dollars bills for the broke ass niggas because coming to the stage is Cinnamon," The DJ yelled.

The crowd went wild. I quickly ordered another drink as Cinnamon sauntered onto the stage. She wore a purple and white halter neck suspender Teddy that showcased all the body she knew men lusted over. I had to admit that she had me in her Charlotte's web at one point but not anymore.

She immediately grabbed the pole and began swaying from side to side. She swung her body gracefully around the pole and stopped midair and began popping her ass up and down. Customers began raining money onto the stage. Cinnamon placed her feet down on the stage and placed the pole between her ass cheeks. She bent over and began twerking.

Her ass cheeks were moving in a wave like motion. She turned around, sticking her pointer finger into her mouth as continued to twerk and smile seductively. The stage was littered with money. She then seductively climbed up the pole, slowing sliding down with her legs in a V shape position. Tons of dollar bills decorated the stage. I turned around with my back facing her because I wanted to run up on stage and snatch that bitch by her hair. I ordered another drink and made a mental note that this would be my last drink. I promised my baby that I would act right and make it home and I was going to do just that.

When Cinnamon's set was over, I turned around and watched her bend over and retrieve her money. Customers grabbed at her feet and legs and security immediately rushed them warning them that if it continued, they would be escorted out.

"I need to holla at Cinnamon," I said downing the last bit of contents left of my drink.

"Alright bro, holla if you need us. You know we stay ready bruh," said Boobie.

"Yo," I replied, walking off in the direction of Cinnamon.

Before I could catch up to her, a nigga approached her and they began having a heated conversation. I couldn't tell what was being said because of how loud the damn music was but I stood back, waiting my turn to confront her. Before I knew it, the nigga had rushed her and began hitting her repeatedly in the face as if she was a nigga! Blood spewed from her once beautiful, well kept, blemish free face. Security rushed the attacker as quickly as possible but that didn't stop the damage that was already done. She had lost a fuckin' tooth!

There was so much chaos that I started to feel uneasy. Shit like this made a nigga paranoid. I had left home without my fye and silently cursed myself for doing so. Cinnamon was on the ground, crying as she bled from her face. My niggas walked up to me asking what happened.

"What the fuck bro," Big Man asked confusingly.

"I'm just as confused as you," I said slowly walking up. With all the chaos going on, I casually walked over to Cinnamon, bent down and took three one hundred dollars bills from her. She glanced up at me, holding out her hand for help. I stuffed the money in my pocket and with a scowl on my face, turned around and walked back to my niggas. That'll teach her!

Chapter 10

Zarela

I had just finished putting Cassandra and Mayur to bed and let me tell you, two kids is definitely hard work but I was already falling for Cassandra. I glanced at the clock and it was almost one in the morning. Cadel had left my house around three in the afternoon. I shook my head, wanting to cry, believing things would change between us. He called me when he got to the club but never texted me while he was there or when he supposedly left.

I decided to hop in the shower. It had been a long day and I was starting to get a headache. I turned on the hot water knob and immediately steamed engulfed the room. I undressed out of one of Cadel's old T-shirts and some leggings that I just wore around the house. I walked butt naked into the kitchen and poured myself a small glass of wine. Walking back towards the bathroom with glass in hand, I sat down on the toilet and took a shit. Once I downed the last bit of my wine, I finished up on the toilet and stepped into the shower.

I let the hot water caress my body as I stood in place, thinking about how dumb I was for letting Cadel suck me back into his life. I grabbed my sponge and squeezed a good amount of shower gel onto it. As I began washing my body, I began to visualize how I thought my future with Cadel would be. A tear slipped from my eye when I realized that twenty more minutes had passed and it would almost be two in the morning soon and still no Cadel.

As I turned around to grab my razor to shave my legs, Cadel stood outside the shower, butt ass naked. A huge smile spread across my face. He stepped into the shower as he pulled me into him. "I told you that I would be home, right?"

"I was worried. I thought you had stood me up and things would be a repeat of the past," I admitted.

"Never that. Some shit went down at the club and some dude beat Cinnamon's ass before I could talk to her. I grabbed my money right next to her ass as she was laid out on the floor. Bruh beat her ass so bad that she lost a tooth." I shook my head and grabbed my razor and began shaving my underarms.

"So, you been at the club all this time?" I asked still needing answers.

"Nah, I left and went to play pool with Big Man and my phone died. I'm sorry. A nigga gotta work on calling you and shit when I'm out but I promise you that I was a good boy," he said with an award winning smile since he had his gold grill out. I stared at him with the right side of my mouth twisted up.

"Baby girl, don't be mad. I had to do what I had to do. I ain't no bitch."

"You need to leave that street shit alone. You're better than that. Why can't you see that?" I asked.

"I know but look stop trying to find a reason to be mad with a nigga. I'm home. I ain't drunk and I'm good. Gimmie a kiss," he asked as he gently pulled the razor from out of my hand. I turned around and did just that. I kissed him so deep and passionate. I wanted to reward him for doing right because for so long he had done wrong.

I dropped down to my knees and took him into my mouth. Water from the shower head rained down on my hair. Cadel looked down at me as I began to suck his third leg like a lollipop. It wasn't long before it swelled more in size. Saliva seeped from the corners of my mouth and by the sounds of him grunting and pulling on my hair, I could tell that he was enjoying this just as much as me. Not wanting to ejaculate, Cadel pulled himself out of my mouth and helped me to my feet.

He turned me around so that my hands were placed on the cold wet bathtub tile. He leaned onto my back as he began to kiss my neck. I felt his dick waiting to enter my sweet center as it lightly tapped against it.

"I love you Zarela. I told you that I was going to do right baby."

"I love you too. I want us to work," I moaned.

"We will girl, now take this dick," Cadel murmured while he entered me from the back.

~

Things had been going so well between Cadel and me. Three weeks had passed and Cadel had terminated his lease at his bachelor pad apartment. Yep, it was official. We were moving in together, well he was moving in with me. I couldn't be happier. I watched as Cadel brought box after box into the apartment. I was noticing the amazing change in him.

He worked, came home, tended to the kids, cleaned and even had been cooking even though he wasn't the best cook. When he was away from me, he would call and keep me informed. I often had to pinch myself because I couldn't believe that this was true. Today was also Gabriela's wedding. I was so excited for my best friend and couldn't wait to see her walk down the aisle. She was just now beginning to show but good thing her dress had still fit.

"Babe, you know I have to run. I can't be late for Gaby's wedding ceremony because you know she'll kill me! I whipped up a homemade lasagna and it's in the oven. Take it out in five minutes. I'll call you later." I leaned in and kissed Cadel on the cheek.

"Alright gurl, have fun," he said smothering Cassandra with kisses as he sat down next to Mayur on the sofa who was watching SpongeBob.

~

I arrived at the church in just enough time. Gabriela was already blowing my phone up. I briskly walked inside the same church that Gaby had Pumpkin's funeral at. Upon entering, Gabriela immediately ran up to me.

"I've been calling you! I'm a nervous wreck," she confessed like a mad pretty woman.

"I'm on time bestie, chill out!" I joked, hugging her and rubbing her protruding belly.

"Let's get this started, shall we?" I asked.

For about an hour we had got our makeup done. Since Gaby didn't have many friends, she had her old boss Chandra and me as her bridesmaids. Of course, Pumpkin was supposed to be in the wedding but due to unfortunate events, she obviously couldn't. Chandra and I had stunning makeup. We had subtly lined lids, softly blushed cheeks, and a strong wine-colored lip for a beautiful berry look. It matched well with our berry, pink, lace maxi bridesmaid dresses.

Gabriela looked striking with a silver, smoky, fully lined eye with an apricot blush and a nude lip color for a stunning finish. Her gown was to die for! She was rocking a Chiffon slim fit-and-flare gown with embroidered cap sleeves. She had a deep plunging Queen Anne neckline and knotted center in the midriff. The amazing gown had lightly hand-beaded embroidered illusion on the back and had a sweep train.

"Wow, Gabriela you look gorgeous," I said with tears in my eyes.

"Thank you," she said eyeing her growing belly in

her gown. "I can't believe that I'm finally getting married. After all the bullshit with Neron, Kimora, my mother, losing my daughter, I finally found my king. I couldn't be happier that I have a man who has stuck by me through all my bull shit." Gabriela began to get teary eyed just like my ass.

"Awwww," I squealed as I hugged my best friend.

"Uh uh ladies, y'all better pull it together before you ruin your snatched makeup," the makeup artist joked.

We chuckled as we dried our eyes and held it together. The makeup artist rushed over to us and began touching up our makeup, making sure we looked perfect for the ceremony. There was a knock at the door and one of Paul's' groomsman passed Chandra a note. Gabriela stood patiently, looking afraid that something was wrong.

"What's wrong?"

"It's a note," Chandra said. "Would you like me to read it?"

"No, that's okay, I'll read it please," Gabriela said walking towards Chandra. Chandra passed Gaby the note and she unfolded it and began reading it.

"Check under your right wedding shoe," Gaby said aloud.

We all stood in place as Gaby walked over to her wedding shoes. She opened the box and turned over the right heel and read, "You're my friend, you're my love, you're my life, I can't wait to make you're my wife, Paul." Gaby smiled like it was graduation day or as if she won the lottery. I was so happy for her. She was in tears as she cried. The makeup artist kept trying to touch up her makeup but the happy tears kept falling so she stood there, letting Gaby get her joyful tears out.

"Let's go get married!" I shouted hugging my best

friend!

Chapter 11

Zarela

Despite Gabriela not having a lot of family and friends, Paul's family turned out the church and the wedding was beautiful. I stood on the side with Chandra as the pastor began to speak. I momentarily looked across from me and seen Ricardo staring at me irregularly. I couldn't pay him any mind. I needed to focus on my best friend's wedding.

"Dearly beloved, we are gathered here today in the presence of these witnesses, to join Gabriela and Paul in matrimony commended to be honorable among all; and therefore is not to be entered into lightly but reverently, passionately, lovingly and solemnly. Into this estate these two persons present come now to be joined. If anyone can show just cause why they may not be lawfully joined together, let them speak now or forever hold their peace.

Once we noticed that no one wanted to object or felt a type of way. The ceremony continued. It was now time for them to exchange vows. My eyes watered to see how much passion Paul had in his eyes for Gaby.

"Gabriela, you are my best friend. I take you as you are. I promise to love who you are now and who you are yet to become. I promise to listen to you and learn from you, to support you and accept your support. I will celebrate your triumphs and mourn your losses as though they were my own. I will love you and have faith in your love for me, through all our years and all that life may bring us." A single tear slipped from Paul's eye and Gabriela delicately wiped it away.

"I don't know how I can top that," Gaby joked as the attendees laughed.

"I love you unconditionally and without hesitation. I vow to love you, encourage you, trust you, and respect you.

As a family, we will create a home filled with learning, laughter, and compassion. I promise to work with you to foster and cherish a relationship of equality knowing that together we will build a life far better than either of us could imagine alone. Today, I choose you to be my husband. I accept you as you are, and I offer myself in return. I will care for you, stand beside you, and share with you all of life's adversities and all of its joys from this day forward, and all the days of my life."

Paul mouthed the words, "I love you," as he smiled at Gaby. She mouthed "I love you more," back. They then exchanged rings.

"By the power vested in me by the State of Florida, I now pronounce you husband and wife. You may now kiss the bride." Gabriela and Paul shared a nasty passionate kiss as we all hooted, hollered and clapped!

"I present to you Mr. and Mrs. Delgado." They

jumped the broom and walked out.

~

All the attendees then drove to the reception location and I got a call from Cadel.

"Hello," I answered as I maneuvered through traffic.

"Hey baby, I'm on the way," he said.

"I hope Gaby and Paul won't be mad that I invited you to the reception."

"Shit, I ain't got an issue with Paul. I'm over that shit. Look, I'll be there in about ten minutes. I got the gift too," he said.

"Okay, how were the kids?"

"They were cool. I dropped them off to Tawny's," Cadel answered as I pulled into the location parking lot.

I waited for Cadel to pull up as I pulled down my sun visor to check my makeup. I was still on point. Minutes later, Cadel pulled up and got out of the car. My baby looked dapper in a two-piece salt and pepper suit. I had re-twisted his dreads a few days ago and they were neatly tied into a ponytail. I stepped out of the car and greeted him with a hug and kiss. We slowly walked up to the building, hand in hand.

The theme was movies, so there was a photo booth set up right outside of the entrance. Cadel and I posed for a quick picture, throwing up the deuces and was handed our copy. We walked inside and the place was jumping. Gabriela immediately spotted us and whispered something to Paul. I nudged Cadel to get his attention and we walked over to the bride and groom table.

"Gabriela, before you speak, just hear me out, please. I know Cadel and Paul have had their differences but with the wedding and everything, we haven't had a chance to catch up."

"I can take it from here Rel. Look I didn't come here to cause problems. I finally got custody of my daughter Cassandra. I'm right now fighting custody to get her twin sister Courtney which isn't mine. As you know, you and Pumpkin were sisters, which make my girls your nieces. I wanna put this bull shit to the side so we can all be cordial and keep that shit one hundred."

Gabriela began to tear up. She had no idea that Cadel went for custody of the girls. She mentioned to me on many occasions how she felt guilty that she wouldn't get to know her nieces. With having custody and caring for her three brothers, her son, daughter and pregnant, she just couldn't take on two twins. Paul sat with a scowl as he slowly stood up. Cadel took a step back, ready for whatever. Paul reached across the table for a champagne glass.

"Paul, what are you doing?" Gaby asked as she and I stood confused. Paul picked up the glass filled with the bubbly liquid and extended it to Cadel, smirking.

"It's all good man," Paul confessed.

Cadel reluctantly grabbed the glass and nodded his head as the two slapped hands.

"Let's enjoy the reception. Everything is cool," Paul added.

It was a huge relief to know that they had officially squashed their beef. Gaby still had tears in her eyes to know that she was officially an aunt. I gently grabbed the Delgado's wedding gift and handed it to them. It was nicely wrapped. Unbeknownst to them it was a personalized chrome frame that said, "Mr. and Mrs. Delgado, happily ever after; Paul and Gabriela."

We partied the night away and had a blast. Ricardo

was there only he kept his distance from us. He gave me a few glances and stares but after the ass whopping Cadel gave him and by it being his brother's wedding, I knew he wouldn't say anything or pop off. I hated how things ended between us but I believe everything worked out for a reason.

I think Ricardo was placed into my life to show me how I was supposed to be treated. As sad as it is to say, he was seasonal. Even seasonal situations can bring with them lessons that last a lifetime. We can all agree that certain types of clothing aren't appropriate year-round, right? We don't wear mittens during summer and we don't wear tank tops in the snow. Depending on the weather, certain clothes don't seem fit and may leave us feeling too hot or too cold. The same can go for relationships.

If the love doesn't last, it prepares you for the one that will. Being with Ricardo showed me that I deserved nothing but the best and I was glad that Cadel was living up to that standard so far. I believed whatever was meant to be was going to be. I believed the man that I was dancing with was the man that I was supposed to be with.

After a few hours we said our goodbyes to a drunken Paul and sober Gabriela since she no longer drank. Cadel and I were feeling good too, quite tipsy as we walked to the parking lot. I drove behind Cadel and followed him home.

Cadel pulled into a parking spot at his new home, my apartment. I pulled up next to him in another vacant spot. I stepped out of the car and walked up to Cadel. Together, we walked up the flight of stairs to the front door. I pulled out my key and inserted it into the key hole.

"Now you know I've been meaning to ask you for a copy of the house key. How a nigga live here but ain't got key," he laughed.

"I got you. The spare is inside my jewelry box. I'll

get it for you once we get inside," I opened the front door and we walked inside.

"Mane, the reception was lit baby," Cadel said taking off his jacket to his suit and sitting down on the sofa.

"It was. I was surprised that Gaby and Paul were cool with me inviting you since I hadn't mentioned it to either one of them. She looked beautiful," I said taking off my heels and walking into my bedroom to grab the spare key for Cadel.

Once I grabbed the spare key from out of my jewelry box, I walked back into the living room and passed the key to Cadel. "That's what's up. Thank you."

"No problem," I said leaning my head onto his shoulder after I sat down next to him.

Seconds later, my cell phone chirped, alerting me of a notification. I sat up and reached over onto the coffee table and grabbed my phone. I entered in my cell phones identification safety pin and used my thumb to pull down my notifications on my phone.

"What in the hell?" I said out loud.

"What's up?" Cadel asked as he grabbed the remote to turn the TV on. He began channel surfing.

I couldn't believe that Cinnamon just sent me a friend request on Facebook. I clicked on her profile and felt the anger build up in my face. There bright as day was a video featuring her and Cadel. Instead of saying anything to him, I clicked on the video. I immediately heard Cadel's voice as soon as I pressed play.

"Yeah, look at all that ass," Cadel said in the video as they laid in bed together and he repeatedly smacked her ass, making it jiggle.

Cadel instantaneously turned the TV off and looked

at me. "What the fuck are you watching?" Instead of responding to him, I continued to watch the video. Cadel began placing kisses on her ass cheeks as Cinnamon continued to record, smiling into the camera. I pressed pause on the video.

"Zarela, what's up? Mane, what are you watching?"

"Cinnamon sent me a friend request. I click on her page and it appears to be a sex tape you made with her! How could you do something like this Cadel? Do you not know shit like this follows you around Ray J?" I yelled.

"Let me see," he asked.

"No, you made the shit, so you should remember," I said sarcastically.

I pressed play on the video and Cinnamon propped whatever up that she was using to record the video and turned her back to the camera, taking off her bra. Without exposing anything, she pulled down Cadel's boxers and proceeded to go down on him. Cadel could be heard grunting as Cinnamon begins making slobbering noises. She must've had whatever device that was recording on a timer because video then ends.

I tossed my phone into Cadel's lap and stood up. I stared at him wishing that I was burning a hole into his head. Cadel pressed play on the video and began watching it. I walked into my bedroom to change out of my bridesmaid dress. I was irritated. I couldn't be mad at the fact that they made a tape or whatever when we weren't together but I was mad that the bitch felt the need to reach out to me just because she wanted to be petty and have me see it. I didn't understand why Cadel always messed with these messy hoes. Seconds later, Cadel walked into the room.

"Listen, that tape was made when we were in Miami. We weren't together," Cadel pleaded. He tossed my phone on the bed. I retrieved it and hit deny on Cinnamon's friend request. I then set my profile picture of an old picture of Cadel and I took together. A picture spoke a thousand words so there was no need for me to respond to her ass.

"I know that. I know it's not something you've done since we've got back together. Especially since you told me what went down at the strip club with her the other day. I just hate seeing you with other women. You always mess with these groupie dirty bitches. Why couldn't you mess with a librarian, a doctor or a business owner," I smirked, trying to lighten the mood.

"Look, that chick just mad that we ain't together. Shit after what I saw at the club, I wasn't the only one she did dirty. The hoe just mad," he said walking up to me and kissing me on the neck. He lightly pushed me on the bed.

"Oh you trying to get something started huh?" I giggled.

"Shit, I might be," he said removing my panties.

"Let me show you how to make a real movie," I teased.

Chapter 12

Cadel

"Bruh, I'm telling you, my third baby mama is nagging a nigga for some child support. I just wanna move and get a new identity," said Lil Step.

We were chilling in the trap and I was counting my money. Rela still didn't know that I had this shit on the side. I didn't tell anybody shit. The more people you told, the messier it could be.

"Mane, you need to start your own line of condoms," Boobie suggested. We all broke out in laughter.

"Fuck y'all. The shit don't feel good wearing one," Lil step added ignorantly as he sipped some lean.

"Shit, a few moments of pleasure could turn into a baby or even something you can't get rid of bruh," I said licking my fingers to continue counting my money.

"I ain't trying to hear all that," Lil Step added. "I ain't caught shit yet."

"Mane shut up! You sound stupid as fuck," Big Man said as he walked by to sit down next to me.

"Whatever," Lil Step yelled as he waved his hand, dismissing us. I shook my head. Some folks could be so uneducated in sex safe.

"Alright, well everything is all here. I'mma re-up next week because shit is selling beautifully. Keep that shit up y'all. I'mma holla at y'all. I gotta get outta here," I said dapping all my boys.

I walked outside and jumped in my truck. Upon starting it, my cell phone rang. It was my baby Z. "Hey baby gurl, what's up?"

"Cadel," she cried out.

"What's wrong? Are you okay? Are the kids good?" I asked sitting up straightly in my seat.

"Its—it's my dad. He had a heart attack! I'm on my way to the hospital now. I'm so scared," she confessed through tears.

"What hospital?"

"Orange Park Medical," she answered quickly.

"I'm on my way! Can you drive? Do I need to come get you?" I was hauling ass down the street.

"No, I'm already on the way. I'll meet you there. I'm so scared."

"I know baby. Everything will be okay. I'll see you when I get there," I said.

I drove like a bat out of hell to the west side. I hoped her father was going to be alright. I knew how close she was to him. I know that he didn't care for me because of all the wrongdoing I've done in her life, but I was a

changed man. No matter how much her pops disliked me, I

wouldn't wish anything bad to happen to him.

~

I arrived at the hospital and rushed inside. I hated

how hospitals smelled and how bland they looked. A nigga

felt like I needed to bubble wrap myself because walking

into a hospital made me feel like I was covered in germs. I

called Zarela and asked her what floor and room number

her father was on. Once she gave me the information, I

made my way to the elevator.

Once on the correct floor, I walked towards ICU. I

lightly knocked on the room door and slowly pushed open

the cracked door. There sat Zarela next to his bed in a plush

chair, holding her father's hand. My heart broke. Seeing her

father laying there with all of those tubes coming out of

him really blew me away.

"How is he?" I whispered to Rela. She looked up at me with the most painful expression I've ever seen. Tears formed in her eyes as she tried to speak but nothing would come out. I walked over to her and kneeled down so I was eye level with her.

"Baby, what did the doctor say?" I asked once again.

"He had a—a massive heart attack Cadel," Rela whimpered.

"Damn. Is he gonna be okay?"

Before she could answer a doctor walked in. He immediately greeted me with a warm welcoming smile. "Hi. I'm doctor Fluttenburg and you are?" He asked holding out his hand.

"Cadel, Zarela's husband," I lied, shaking his hand.

"Nice to meet you," he said walking over to Cornel, Rela's father.

"Will he recover? What caused this?" I asked, nervous to know the answer. I stuffed my hands in my pockets, prepared to hear the worse.

"Cornel here had a massive heart attack. Heart attacks occur when there is a blockage in one or more of the arteries to the heart, preventing the heart from receiving enough oxygen-rich blood. If the oxygen in the blood cannot reach the heart muscle, the heart becomes damaged. He was fortunate that his daughter found him when she did. We have to run some tests to see the extent that the damage has or might have caused so I can't really say much more. He's on medication at this moment, therefore, he's unresponsive right now but I assure you we're going to do everything in our power to help your father in law."

"Thank you. Preciate it."

The doctor looked at some monitors and poked around a bit before he excused himself and left. The only sounds that could be heard in the room were the sound of monitors beeping and Zarela crying. I walked over to her, pulled her up from her chair and just hugged her.

Chapter 13

Zarela

I couldn't believe that my father had a heart attack, a massive one at that. I remember finding him. I went to pick up Mayur and when I used my spare key to unlock his front door, I found him slumped over the kitchen table and Mayur crying in the highchair. I panicked at first, just standing there screaming but I quickly regained composure and dialed 911. I shook my head to get the horrible memory out of my head as I sat next to my father. He was recovering and making some progress. He finally spoke today and asked for a beer! I smirked when I thought about my father's first words.

"Daddy, you know that you scared me right?" I asked, holding his hand and rubbing the top of his hand with my thumb. I hadn't left the hospital in three days. I called out of work while Cadel took care of the kids and brought me clothes to the hospital.

"I'm sorry. Your old man needs to take better care of myself," he said in a raspy tone.

"You really do, because I need you, dad. I need you," I cried out.

"Shhh, it is okay, Zarela. I'll be okay," he said giving me a faint smile. I wiped my tears, sniffled and cleared my throat.

"The doctor said that you'll be released in two days. You also need to watch your cholesterol intake daddy, start eating healthier and living a better lifestyle. I probably need to find Mayur a daycare because I think sometimes it's too much for you to watch your grandson," I confessed as I stared at him with loving eyes.

"I know I need to do better but you will do no such thing as to take Mayur from me. You know I love my grandson, so nonsense," he said getting upset.

"Okay, daddy, relax," I said standing up and looking down at him.

"I was just saying that I might not let you watch him as much as before. I didn't say that I would take him away from you," I tried to clarify.

"Well, it's pretty much the same to me. Reducing my grandpa time sure sounds like taking him away from me and you will do no such thing. I'm still as sharp as a tack. You heard the doc," he said grinning.

"You're so stubborn," I said leaning down and kissing my father on the forehead.

The sound of the room door opening caught our attention. We looked over towards the door and Cadel walked in with "Get Well Soon" balloons. I smiled at how supportive he was during this difficult time for me. Gaby had come by to see my dad yesterday but she didn't stay long since she was on bed rest for some slight cramping but she and the baby were doing just fine. Cadel walked over to my dad and sat the balloons down on the floor. They were held down by a weight.

"How are you Mr. Cornel?" Cadel asked with a smile.

"I'm still alive and kicking man. Thanks for the balloons," my dad said.

"No problem. I didn't know what to bring for a playa like yourself," Cadel joked, causing us all to laugh. He walked around the bed and kissed me on the cheek. He started to look nervous and I wasn't sure why he was looking kind of off.

"Are you alright?" I asked above a whisper. I couldn't take the other best man in my life to be admitted to the hospital.

"I'm good Rel, I'm straight. Um—look, I know I'm doing this wrong but I felt this was the best way seeing as to how Big C is here. Mr. Cornel, I wish things could've been different but I would like to ask for your daughter's hand in marriage," he asked nervously. He swallowed a big gulp. I've never seen him this nervous before.

"Is this real?" I asked bringing my hands up to cover my mouth.

"You know--," my father started off before he started coughing. I rushed to his side and grabbed the small plastic cup of water. I brought the cup to his lips as he slowly sipped water from out of the straw.

"Thank you baby girl, help me sit up a bit will ya?" I helped my father to sit up and began fluffing some pillows. My father began speaking again.

"When you two first started dating, I'll be honest I didn't like you."

"I didn't like myself either," Cadel interrupted.

"Let me finish son," my dad said. Cadel threw his hands up in the air.

"A father always wants his baby girl to end up with a man that will love, honor, respect and cherish her. You didn't do any of those things, but for some reason my daughter was still fond of you and loved you. You then got her pregnant and dogged her out even more. She gave you chance after chance and you still disrespected her," my father took a deep breath before he began speaking again. I was getting nervous about where this conversation was going.

"But one thing I know, I've always supported my daughter. I can't protect her anymore since she's grown. When she told me that you two were getting back together, I was pissed. I'm not gonna lie but lately, all she's been telling me is how much you've changed and how good you've been to her. Love is not about how much you say I love you. It's about how much you can prove that it's true love. You have my blessing." My father smiled and nodded his head at Cadel.

"Thank you sir, I really am going to do right by her. I have been doing right by her." Cadel turned towards me and grinned. He slowly walked towards me and got on one knee. My heart instantly pounded. For a second, I felt like *I* was about to have a damn heart attack.

"Zarela, I want to see your wrinkled face sitting right in my chair when we get old, reading a book on that damn Kindle. I would rather spend one lifetime with your ass – than face all the ages of this world alone. I love you not only for what you are but for what a nigga is when I'm with you. I can't imagine my life without you gurl. I love you simply because you are my life and that's all I have to say because you know a nigga ain't good with words." Cadel quickly covered his mouth. "Excuse my language Mr. C." My dad laughed and threw his hand down in the air to let him know that it was okay.

"Look—Zarela, will you be my wife?" He reached into his pocket and pulled out a beautiful, 1/4 carrot, round-cut, 10K White Gold diamond engagement ring. I was in awe at how well it sparkled. It was stunning. I was speechless.

"Will you marry me?" Cadel asked again, interrupting my thoughts.

"Yessss, yesss I'll marry you!" I screamed! Cadel slid the ring on my finger and stood up. I leaped into his arms, wrapping my legs around his waist. I began planting kisses all over his face as my father clapped from his hospital bed.

"Wow, it's beautiful," I said once Cadel placed me on my feet. My ring was breathtaking. I couldn't stop admiring it.

"Thank you. I picked it out myself," he said proudly as he cheesed like a big ass kid. I held my hand up into the air, admiring my ring from afar. He did *well*!

"I love you Zarela and I promise that I'll love you the right way for the rest of your life."

"I love you too," I said pecking him on the lips and running over to my father to show him the ring.

"Well, I'm sorry that I have to run but I gotta get to work. Tawny is watching the kids. I'll call you later." He kissed me again and told my dad goodbye and walked out the door.

"It's absolutely beautiful baby girl," he said weakly.

"You need to rest daddy. I'mma stretch out on the couch," I said as I dimmed the lights in the hospital room.

My father didn't say another word as he quickly drifted off to sleep. I walked over to the uncomfortable couch and sat down. My phone vibrated inside my purse. I thought it was a text from Cadel but to my surprise, it was another notification from Cinnamon's annoying ass on Facebook. This time she left a message. I blew air from my lips before I clicked on the message to read it.

"I'm pregnant. I've been trying to reach Cadel but he's ignoring me. Please let him know that it's his baby and I'm keeping it."

I wanted to drop my phone. Why was it whenever Cadel and I were doing great, some chick had to swoop in and take my joy? It was as if she was a fly on the wall. I had been engaged for less than thirty minutes and already new drama had popped up. I immediately began thinking, what if Cadel knew that she was pregnant and only proposed because he knew that she was? What if this engagement was not because he loved me but because he was guilty? I immediately felt sick to my stomach. I jumped up from the couch and ran into the restroom that was inside daddy's room. Closing the door quickly, I hurled all of my breakfast into the toilet. I flopped down on the cold hard tile and cried.

Chapter 14

Cadel

I had just clocked out from work and was anxious like hell to talk to Rela. I had been texting her throughout the day and even called her on my break and she hadn't responded or returned my call. I started to get worried. I walked towards my truck and decided to try and call her again. When her voicemail picked up, I hung up.

I drove twenty over the speed limit all the way home. When I pulled into her—I mean our complex, I noticed she was home. I instantly became confused. I was barely able to put my car into park when I hopped out of my truck, almost busting my ass. I sprinted up the stairs, two by two as I had my key ready in my hand. Swiftly inserting my key, I heard the lock click and I turned the knob practically swinging open the door like a mad man.

When I entered our apartment, I found Rela curled up on the sofa with her Kindle Fire in her hand. I instantly became pissed when I saw that she had placed her engagement ring on the coffee table. To see that shit wasn't wrong with her had my blood boiling. After I just proposed to this woman, she ignores me and then has the nerve to take off the ring that I had just placed on her finger. What the fuck did I do?

"Yo, what in the entire fuck is wrong with chu?" I asked, yelling to the top of my lungs. She looked up at me with swollen, puffy eyes.

"I've been calling you, are you alright? Yo pops good? Where are the kids? Why does it look like you've been crying Rel?" I was tossing out questions like a pop quiz.

"The kids are fine. I just put them down for a nap. My dad is fine. It's you who isn't!" Rela put down her

Kindle and stood up. She crossed her arms over her chest and stared at me.

"What is yo problem? You got my ring on the table? What you having second thoughts about marrying a nigga?"

"Cinnamon sent me a message and she's pregnant by you! Did you know that?" She asked with hurt in her voice. I was shocked hearing her say these words to me but I knew that I had nothing but safe sex with Cinnamon. That wasn't my damn baby!

"That's why yo ass tripping? Mane that damn stupid ass girl ain't pregnant woe. I strapped up every time with that damn girl. I bought my own condoms and always rolled them on. She couldn't try any funny shit with me even if she tried. I made sure I was strapped with that hoe," I said honestly. Zarela's shoulders slumped down as she slowly walked towards me.

186

"Do you promise that it's not your baby?" She asked again.

"Mane on my life it ain't my baby and I believe that there ain't no damn baby to begin with. That chick already lost custody of her kid. Don't nobody wanna knock her ass up," I said truthfully. When Zarela didn't respond, I continued running my mouth.

"Now stop fuckin' tripping and put my ring back on," I said walking over to the coffee table, picking up the engagement ring and slipping it back on her finger.

"We doing this shit right. Ain't any time for games. We've been there and done that but for future reference, don't ignore me like you did today. We're about to get married. All that immature bull shit is dead. You're about to be my wife. You better come to a nigga when you have a question or an issue with a me. I thought something was wrong with you when I didn't hear from your ass today and then to see you were straight, I wanted to ring your neck!" I joked.

"I'm sorry. I guess I'm so used to shit always fuckin' up that I sometimes feel that things are going so great between us because it's too good to be true," she confessed as she wrapped her arms around my neck.

"That ain't nothing but the devil. For each new level in life is a new devil. We're gonna be all right baby girl. Believe dat! Now go ahead and update that Facebook status to taken. All Cinnamon is mad about is that I left her ass and I'm back with you. A woman like her hates to feel dismissed and rejected. She doesn't know how to take it."

"You're right! I'm sorry that I doubted you baby."

She kissed me intensely on the lips, sliding in some tongue as I palmed her ass. Once we broke our kiss, she grabbed her phone from off of the table and clicked on the

Facebook icon on her phone. Within seconds, she updated her relationship status to "engaged." She then took a picture of her engagement ring and hit post. Within seconds her notifications blew up with "Congrats" and "Wow, your ring is beautiful."

"I blocked Cinnamon as well," she added as she snickered and pulled me by the arm into our bedroom.

"Let's get a quickie in before the kids wake up," she said sneakily, biting her bottom lip.

~

We had just finished our quickie and my cell phone rang from inside my pants pocket. I swung my feet over the bed and bent down to grab my pants that were by my feet. I reached into my pocket and pulled out my cell phone. It was Rosie.

"Hello," I answered out of breath from the fuck session I just had with Zarela.

"Hi, this is Rosie. How are you Cadel?" She asked chipper.

"I'm fine. How are you?"

"I'm great," she responded.

"Any news on Courtney?" I asked eagerly. Zarela sat up in bed, pulling the sheets up to her bellybutton.

"That's actually why I'm calling. Everything has checked out and Courtney is ready to come home to you!" I felt like a million bucks hearing that my daughter was ready to come home. Yep, my daughter. It didn't matter that biologically, she wasn't mine. She was now mine and I was going to be there for her just like Mayur and Cassandra.

"Wow, this is great. Thank you so much, Rosie. You've been amazing. When can I come pick her up?" I asked eagerly. I glanced at Zarela and she smiled widely, happy for me and that our home would be expanding.

"Tomorrow morning will be great! Well, I don't want to hold you any longer. I'll see you tomorrow," she said cheerfully.

"I'll be there. Thank you again," I said before we disconnected.

A nigga felt like a million bucks. I had my girl, my daughters and my son. I was a blessed man.

Chapter 15

Cadel

Four months later….

We were having a barbecue for Mayur's birthday in our new home. I was blessed to score us a home with three bedrooms, two bathrooms all one thousand, eight hundred and ninety-three square feet. The house was super fuckin' dope & immaculate too! It had a beautiful brick fireplace in our large family room with soaring vaulted ceilings!

Our kitchen was huge with Viking appliances. Our kitchen even had a cozy breakfast nook overlooking our charming & peaceful large backyard. I updated our kitchen and bathrooms with updated custom cabinets, solid surface countertops & tile floors. The large master bedroom also had vaulted ceilings. The front yard was large and fenced in for the kids to play around in. Did I mention that we lived in a safe, desirable and quiet, secluded neighborhood in Mandarin? We lived in the perfect family environment.

Zarela walked into the kitchen looking beautiful in some skinny jeans with a BeBe shirt. She had finally straightened her natural hair with a blowout. It was bone straight with a part down the middle. Her hair stopped right in the middle of her back. It was so long and healthy that one would think that my baby was rocking a weave.

"Hey Mrs. Wright," I teased as I walked up to her and kissed her on the cheek.

I married my baby in front of Paul, her pops, Gabriela and my boys, Big Man, Boobie and Lil Step last month at the courts. We both didn't want to have anything big. We just wanted the people that matter the most to be there. We had bigger goals to achieve which was using the money we would've used on a big wedding towards our dream home that we just purchased. If my woman was happy, I was happy.

"Baby can you grab the potato salad please," Rela asked.

"You know that I can boo," I said chugging down my Crown Royal. I tucked the Crown Royal bottle underneath my arm as I grabbed the potato salad that my baby made. We walked outside and it was beautiful. The sun was shining brightly as I placed the two big bowls of potato salad on our picnic table that we had in our backyard.

"Looks damn good son," said Cornel as he stood up from a patio chair. I noticed his cup was empty so I took the liquor bottle and poured the liquor into his empty plastic red cup.

"You better slow down daddy! You know you aren't supposed to be drinking after your heart attack, you promised me," Rela butted in.

"I know but it's a special occasion and it's my grandson's birthday," he tried to reason as he popped open a can of Sprite to mix with his Crown Royal.

Zarela shook her head as she glanced at the twins who were now seven months. They were learning how to pull up on things, trying to stand up. They were absolutely beautiful. We watched as the clown we hired performed balloon tricks for Gaby's kids, brothers and Mayur. They were so into it as he made different animals out of balloons.

Gay waddled over towards us a she rubbed her gigantic belly. Her shit looked like something out of Star Trek! She was only seven months but looked like if you took a safety pin and tapped her stomach it would pop.

"My nieces are so funny! I was trying to get them to say Titi but all they keep saying is Dada," she said through laughter. Zarela walked up and rubbed her belly as she felt her baby kick.

"I can't wait to meet her," Rela beamed.

"Girl you and me both! I'm as big as a house," she said slowly squatting down to sit down.

"How's the new house man?" I asked Paul.

"Beautiful man. It's not as big as y'all place with square feet but I'm grateful that we found a four bedroom home so everyone is comfortable. Gaby and I have our own room, Magdalena and the new baby will share a room, the three youngest boys will share a room and Gabriela's oldest brother will have his own room because he's like what?" Paul asked as he looked at Gaby for an answer.

"Fifteen now," Gabriela answered with a smirk as she shook her head.

"Shit, I can't keep up! Anyway, with eight people, it was needed man," Paul said taking a swig of his drink.

"I hear that. I'm ready to fill this house up with some more babies," I said glancing at Rela and winking. She giggled as she sat down.

"So, you know Ricardo moved to California? He got a really good job offer. He sends his congratulations on the new house and told me to give you all this card." Gabriela passed Zarela the sealed envelope. Zarela shot me a quick glance and sat down the card.

"Look mane, that shit got out of hand when Ricardo and I fought bruh. He was talking big shit and I was talking big shit," I said sternly to Paul. I knew he and I squashed the beef so I wanted to make sure everything was still cool, especially while he was in my house.

"Mane it's water under the bridge. Ricardo said he's good and over it. We had our beef and I'm Gucci bruh. We gotta be civil for these kids," Paul said honestly.

"That's what's up. Real nigga shit," I said pumping fists with Paul.

"Well damn, I wish bitches got rid of beef as quickly as men could," Gabriela said. "Sorry for cursing Mr. Cornel, but it's the truth," she added. We all belted into laughter. Cornel just shook his head, feeling good on that liquor.

"That's because y'all women are stubborn. Y'all always wanna be right," Paul added. I nodded my head in agreement.

"Whatever," Zarela said smirking.

"So what's up with that bitch Cinnamon?" Gabriela asked?

Zarela's dad just smirked and shook his head as he sipped his drink, listening to our gossip.

"Hell if we know. I blocked her and haven't heard from her since. The hell with her," Rela said making herself a drink.

"Let's cheers to my son who's celebrating another birthday today," Rela said raising her cup in the air.

Chapter 16

Zarela

I woke up with a crazy hangover after Mayur's birthday party. I decided to let Cadel sleep and make some breakfast. I swung my feet over my bed and yawned. I couldn't believe I had slept this late. Even the kids were still knocked out and it was almost one in the afternoon.

I dragged myself to the bathroom to wash my face. I looked horrible. Those shots of Crown Royal knocked me on my ass. I quickly brushed my teeth, gagging from the smell of the toothpaste. I needed to get some food in my body and quick.

I shuffled into my kitchen and rummaged through some pots and pans. I was about to throw down! I whipped up some scrambled eggs, hash browns, sausage patties, bacon and French toast. As I was preparing plates, the sound of the doorbell stopped me dead in my tracks. I wrapped my robe around my body and trotted to my front door. I peeked out the peephole and it was UPS. I opened the door.

"Mrs. Wright?" The UPS deliveryman asked.

"Yes?"

"I have a delivery for you. Please sign here." I hastily signed the electronic clipboard and the UPS man walked back to his truck and put two huge boxes on his dolly. I yelled for Cadel because the boxes were so huge and I knew that the UPS man wasn't allowed to enter people's homes because of policy. Within seconds Cadel dashed to the front of the house, rubbing the sleep from his eyes.

"Oh, it's here," he said bringing the boxes into our house as he thanked the deliveryman.

"What's this?" I asked, eyeing him.

"Our new King bed, we needed a new one. A nigga ain't comfortable sleeping on your shit after you been with another man woe. This is a new bed, for a new start as husband and wife."

"Aw, that's a great idea baby," I said excitedly.

My cell phone ringing put our mini celebration to a halt. I raced towards my phone and saw Gabriela's name flashing. I rapidly answered. "Hello, are you okay?"

"Noooooo, my water broke and I'm in labor! Meet me at Baptist Beaches," she squealed.

"Okay, I'm on my way," I shouted as we hung up on our call.

"She's in labor," I shouted!

"Go get dressed baby. I'll take everything from here." Cadel didn't have to tell me anything twice. I raced into our bedroom and tossed on some Victoria Secret Pink pants and a plain white shirt. I slipped my feet into some white AirMax. I then tied my messy hair into a ponytail.

"I'll call you with an update baby," I yelled as I closed the front door behind me.

~

"Push Gabriela, push," I yelled!

"Argggggghhhhh," Gabriela yelled and grunted as she strained and pushed.

"I see the head," I blurted out as I placed my right hand over my mouth. Tears began to form in my eyes as I witnessed my best friend giving birth.

"Keep pushing Mrs. Delgado. Look, look down," said the nurse calmly and cheerfully. Gabriela looked down with beads of sweat on her forehead and her hair curly on her edges from sweating profusely. Her eyes lit up when she saw her daughters head poking up at her with her eyes closed.

"Oh my God," she cried out as Paul stood by her side. Her daughter had so much hair! She was beautiful and she technically wasn't even born yet.

"One more push Gabriela," said her doctor. Gabriela pushed one more hard time and her daughter Leilani was born! Paul quickly cut the cord and kissed his wife while their daughter wailed. The doctor delivered the placenta while the nurses cleaned up Leilani.

"Seven pounds even, twenty-one inches long," shouted a nurse.

"Congratulations bestie, she's beautiful," I said kissing my best friend on the forehead. I briskly walked over to my God daughter as she wailed and turned red from crying. My cell phone vibrated and I noticed that it was

Cadel calling. I excused myself and stepped out in the hallway.

"Hello, baby she had the baby," I squealed into the phone.

"Rela, I'm about to go to jail," Cadel blurted into the receiver. My heart sunk.

"Jail? Why?" I asked above a whisper, afraid of the answer.

"Look, I haven't always been honest. I've always made some extra money on the side by selling dope out of my trap house with my boys. Somebody ratted us out." I heard a lot of commotion going on in the background.

"Where are you? Are you okay?" Too many questions ran through my mind that I couldn't get them out fast enough.

"I just dashed out of my trap house. I'm in my car now. They already got my boys. I just wanted to tell you in case I didn't have a chance to. I'm sorry baby. I should've been honest but I never told anyone that I sold shit on the side outside of my job," he confessed.

I took a deep breath and tightly squeezed my eyes shut.

"I already knew that you were selling *something* on the side because no offense your job didn't pay enough to afford the lifestyle that you live Cadel. Look, I'll hire a lawyer," I said frantically.

"I love you. I gotta go because they're behind me right now." Tears fell from my eyes, not knowing how long he was going to jail or if he was going to be okay. My heart ached for my husband and my kids.

"Step out of the fuckin' car right damn now boy," yelled an officer. I heard police sirens and a ton of yelling.

"I'm stepping out now," I heard Cadel yell back as the call dropped.

I stood there unable to move as I slid down the hospital wall. What did this mean for my kids and me? Was he okay?

~

Six months later...

I was sitting down at my desk after just reading a letter from Cadel. He had just received his sentencing and he was sentenced to one year in jail with time served. Imagine both of our faces when we found out drunk ass Lil Step had fucked Cinnamon and blurted out how he ran a trap with Cadel. Cinnamon couldn't wait to use that information against Cadel. She wasted no time snitching on my husband, along with Lil Step.

He couldn't believe that his own boy would snitch. I had warned him that Lil Step was nothing but a pothead, lean drunk, but you couldn't tell Cadel shit about his boy. Now look at Cadel, Boobie, Big Man and Lil Step, in jail. Big Man took the fall for everything like a G so that everyone else could get off with lesser sentences. He was sentenced to five years without the possibility of parole. Bobbie was sentenced to the same amount of time as Cadel and as for Lil Step, they transferred him since they knew Cadel, Boobie and Big Man had beef with him for accidently snitching.

With Cadel going to jail, it actually brought us closer. It made him realize that nothing else was more important than his family and living right. I rubbed my belly and felt my unborn daughter kick. I was six months pregnant. That day that Cadel called me from the hospital, I freaked out in the hallway and had an anxiety attack. A nurse spotted me and immediately treated me and it was then that I found out I was pregnant.

During my last letter to Cadel, I had finally told him that I was pregnant. I contemplated on telling him because I didn't want him to worry or stress out anymore than he was. I knew he was going to miss the birth and the babies first nine months of life once our daughter Bianca was born. Cadel was so excited that we were finally having another baby regardless of the circumstances.

I studied the drawing that he drew for me in his letter. He had started drawing in jail and was actually pretty good at it. He had mentioned that he wanted to open up a tattoo shop and go one hundred percent legit and legal. I cried as I folded Cadel's letter back up.

I wiped my eyes as I powered on my laptop. I was going to stand by my husband and stick out this sentence with him. I grabbed my notepad and began typing the synopsis for my book. Since Cadel had been away I was writing a fictional book called "My baby daddy is now a man." It dabbled on me and Cadel's relationship and how much he had changed.

I was on the last few chapters and I couldn't wait to shop my book around to publishers. I began typing away as the words for my synopsis flowed. I sat back reading my synopsis out-loud and was damn proud to see how well it sounded.

A father is a provider, a spiritual adviser, a confidant, and a leader of the family. If you're a *man* with children and you're not doing or being those things, you are simply a baby's daddy. Nah, you're an unfaithful baby daddy. That's definitely not a good look. Wake up! Be a *real* father. Children are born into the world out of relations between two adults so they have no say in it. There is no excuse for men, to slack on their responsibilities or to turn their back on their children due to baby mama from hell. Suck it up and realize that children have to be raised

… period! This is my story of being with a man who went

from being an unfaithful baby daddy to a man, a father and

a husband. If he could change his ways, hell anyone's baby

daddy could! It all depends on how much you're willing to

put up with.

The End!!

Thank you for reading!

Read Gaby (Gabriela's) Story Today:

<u>Baby Mama from Hell</u>

<u>Baby Mama from Hell 2</u>

<u>Baby Mama from Hell 3</u>

Please leave a review! Thank you for your purchase!

*

Rikenya Hunter, born in Louisville Kentucky, writes from a young adult's point of view. Rikenya has always had a passion for writing and storytelling and has been keeping a journal of her life since the age of eight. She has a unique way of seeing life through her character's eyes, leading you along the path as a participant instead of an observer. Rikenya currently resides in Jacksonville Florida, with her high-school sweetheart and their two daughters. She recently signed to Niyah Moore Presents .... Ambiance Books. She's currently working on new material and working towards earning her Bachelor's Degree in Business Administration.

To interact with her:

www.RikenyaHunter.com

***

www.Facebook.com/Rikenya

www.Twitter.com/RikenyaXoXo

www.Instagram.com/Rikenyaxoxo

Made in the USA
Middletown, DE
23 April 2017